The Politeness of Princes

And Other School Stories

P.G. Wodehouse

HAWK PRESS

Published by

Hawk Press

4836/24, Ansari Road, Daryaganj
New Delhi – 110 002
Phones : 9643330713, 91-11-23278618, 91-11-35676207
E-mail: thehawkpress@gmail.com
www.thehawkpress.com

Contents

The Politeness Of Princes

The painful case of G. Montgomery Chapple, bachelor, of Seymour's house, Wrykyn. Let us examine and ponder over it.

It has been well said that this is the age of the specialist. Everybody, if they wish to leave the world a better and happier place for their stay in it, should endeavour to adopt some speciality and make it their own. Chapple's speciality was being late for breakfast. He was late not once or twice, but every day. Sometimes he would scramble in about the time of the second cup of coffee, buttoning his waistcoat as he sidled to his place. Generally he would arrive just as the rest of the house were filing out; when, having lurked hidden until Mr. Seymour was out of the way, he would enter into private treaty with Herbert, the factotum, who had influence with the cook, for Something Hot and maybe a fresh brew of coffee. For there was nothing of the amateur late-breakfaster about Chapple. Your amateur slinks in with blushes deepening the naturally healthy hue of his face, and, bolting a piece of dry bread and gulping down a cup of cold coffee, dashes out again, filled more with good resolutions for the future than with food. Not so Chapple. He liked his meals. He wanted a good deal here below, and wanted it hot and fresh. Conscience had but a poor time when it tried to bully Chapple. He had it weak in the first round.

But there was one more powerful than Conscience—Mr. Seymour. He had marked the constant lateness of our hero, and disapproved of it.

Thus it happened that Chapple, having finished an excellent breakfast one morning some twenty minutes after everybody else, was informed as he sat in the junior day-room trying, with the help of an illustrated article in a boys' paper, to construct a handy model steam-engine out of a reel of cotton and an old note-book—for his was in many ways a giant brain—that Mr. Seymour would like to have a friendly chat with him in his study. Laying aside his handy model steam-engine, he went off to the housemaster's study.

"You were late for breakfast to-day," said Mr. Seymour, in the horrid, abrupt way housemasters have.

"Why, yes, sir," said Chapple, pleasantly.

"And the day before."

"Yes, sir."

"And the day before that."

Chapple did not deny it. He stood on one foot and smiled a propitiating smile. So far Mr. Seymour was entitled to demand a cigar or cocoanut every time.

The housemaster walked to the window, looked out, returned to the mantelpiece, and shifted the position of a china vase two and a quarter inches to the left. Chapple, by way of spirited repartee, stood on the other leg and curled the disengaged foot round his ankle. The conversation was getting quite intellectual.

"You will write out——"

"Sir, please, sir——" interrupted Chapple in an "I-represent-the defendant-m'lud" tone of voice.

"Well?"

"It's awfully hard to hear the bell from where I sleep, sir."

Owing to the increased numbers of the house this term Chapple had been removed from his dormitory proper to a small room some distance away.

"Nonsense. The bell can be heard perfectly well all over the house."

There was reason in what he said. Herbert, who woke the house of a morning, did so by ringing a bell. It was a big bell, and he enjoyed ringing it. Few sleepers, however sound, could dream on peacefully through Herbert's morning solo. After five seconds of it they would turn over uneasily. After seven they would sit up. At the end of the first quarter of a minute they would be out of bed, and you would be wondering where they picked up such expressions.

Chapple murmured wordlessly in reply. He realised that his defence was a thin one. Mr. Seymour followed up his advantage.

"You will write a hundred lines of Vergil," he said, "and if you are late again to-morrow I shall double them."

Chapple retired.

This, he felt, was a crisis. He had been pursuing his career of unpunctuality so long that he had never quite realised that a time might come when the authorities would drop on him. For a moment he felt that it was impossible, that he could not meet Mr. Seymour's wishes in the matter; but the bull-dog pluck of the true Englishman caused him to reconsider this. He would at least have a dash at it.

"I'll tell you what to do," said his friend, Brodie, when consulted on the point over a quiet pot of tea that afternoon. "You ought to sleep without so many things on the bed. How many blankets do you use, for instance?"

"I don't know," said Chapple. "As many as they shove on."

It had never occurred to him to reckon up the amount of his bedclothes before retiring to rest.

"Well, you take my tip," said Brodie, "and only sleep with one on. Then the cold'll wake you in the morning, and you'll get up because it'll be more comfortable than staying in bed."

This scientific plan might have worked. In fact, to a certain extent it did work. It woke Chapple in the morning, as Brodie had predicted; but it woke him at the wrong hour. It is no good springing out of bed when there are still three hours to breakfast. When Chapple woke at five the next morning, after a series of dreams, the scenes of which were laid mainly in the Arctic regions, he first sneezed, then he piled upon the bed everything he could find, including his boots, and then went to sleep again. The genial warmth oozed through his form, and continued to ooze until he woke once more, this time at eight-fifteen. Breakfast being at eight, it occurred to him that his position with Mr. Seymour was not improved. While he was devoting a few moments' profound meditation to this point the genial warmth got in its fell work once again. When he next woke, the bell was ringing for school. He lowered the world's record for rapid dressing, and was just in time to accompany the tail of the procession into the form-room.

"You were late again this morning," said Mr. Seymour, after dinner.

"Yes, sir. I overslebbed myselb, sir," replied Chapple, who was suffering from a cold in the head.

"Two hundred lines."

"Yes, sir."

Things had now become serious. It was no good going to Brodie again for counsel. Brodie had done for himself, proved himself a fraud, an idiot. In fine, a rotter. He must try somebody else. Happy thought. Spenlow. It was a cold day, when Spenlow got left behind. He would know what to do. *There* was a chap for you, if you liked! Young, mind you, but what a brain! Colossal!

"What *I* should do," said Spenlow, "is this. I should put my watch on half an hour."

"What 'ud be the good of that?"

"Why, don't you see? You'd wake up and find it was ten to eight, say, by your watch, so you'd shove on the pace dressing, and nip downstairs, and then find that you'd really got tons of time. What price that?"

"But I should remember I'd put my watch on," objected Chapple.

"Oh, no, probably not. You'd be half asleep, and you'd shoot out of bed before you remembered, and that's all you'd want. It's the getting out of bed that's so difficult. If you were once out, you wouldn't want to get back again."

"Oh, shouldn't I?" said Chapple.

"Well, you might want to, but you'd have the sense not to do it."

"It's not a bad idea," said Chapple. "Thanks."

That night he took his Waterbury, prised open the face with a pocket-knife as if he were opening an oyster, put the minute hand on exactly half an hour, and retired to bed satisfied. There was going to be no nonsense about it this time.

I am sorry to disappoint the reader, but facts are facts, and I must not tamper with them. It is, therefore, my duty to state, however reluctantly, that Chapple was not in time for breakfast on the following morning. He woke at seven o'clock, when the hands of the watch pointed to seven-thirty. Primed with virtuous resolutions, he was just about to leap from his couch, when his memory began to work, and he recollected that he had still an hour. Punctuality, he felt, was an excellent thing, a noble virtue, in fact, but it was no good overdoing it. He could give himself at least another half hour. So he dozed off. He woke again with something of a start. He seemed to feel that he had been asleep for a considerable time. But no. A glance at the watch showed the hands pointing to twenty-five to eight. Twenty-five minutes more. He had a good long doze this time. Then, feeling that now he really must be getting up, he looked once more at the watch, and rubbed his eyes. It was still twenty-five to eight.

The fact was that, in the exhilaration of putting the hands on, he had forgotten that other and even more important operation, winding up. The watch had stopped.

There are few more disturbing sensations than that of suddenly discovering that one has no means of telling the time. This is especially so when one has to be in a certain place by a certain hour. It gives the discoverer a weird, lost feeling, as if he had stopped dead while all the rest of the world had moved on at the usual rate. It is a sensation not unlike that of the man who arrives on the platform of a railway station just in time to see the tail-end of his train disappear.

Until that morning the world's record for dressing (set up the day before) had been five minutes, twenty-three and a fifth seconds. He lowered this by two seconds, and went downstairs.

The house was empty. In the passage that led to the dining-room he looked at the clock, and his heart turned a somersault. *It was five minutes past nine.* Not only was he late for breakfast, but late for school, too. Never before had he brought off the double event.

There was a little unpleasantness in his form room when he stole in at seven minutes past the hour. Mr. Dexter, his form-master, never a jolly sort of man to have dealings with, was rather bitter on the subject.

"You are incorrigibly lazy and unpunctual," said Mr. Dexter, towards the end of the address. "You will do me a hundred lines."

"Oo-o-o, sir-r," said Chapple. But he felt at the time that it was not much of a repartee. After dinner there was the usual interview with Mr. Seymour.

"You were late again this morning," he said.

"Yes, sir," said Chapple.

"Two hundred lines."

"Yes, sir."

The thing was becoming monotonous.

Chapple pulled himself together. This must stop. He had said that several times previously, but now he meant it. Nor poppy, nor mandragora, nor all the drowsy syrups of the world should make him oversleep himself again. This time he would try a combination of schemes.

Before he went to bed that night he put his watch on half an hour, wound it up, and placed it on a chair at his bedside. Then he seized his rug and all the blankets except one, and tore them off. Then he piled them in an untidy heap in the most distant corner of the room. He meant to put temptation out of his reach. There should be no genial warmth on this occasion.

Nor was there. He woke at six feeling as if he were one solid chunk of ice. He put up with it in a torpid sort of way till seven. Then he could stand it no longer. It would not be pleasant getting up and going downstairs to the cheerless junior day-room, but it was the only thing to do. He knew that if he once wrapped himself in the blankets which stared at him invitingly from the opposite corner of the room, he was lost. So he crawled out of bed, shivering, washed unenthusiastically, and he proceeded to put on his clothes.

Downstairs it was more unpleasant than one would have believed possible. The day-room was in its usual state of disorder. The fire was not lit. There was a vague smell of apples. Life was very, very grey. There seemed no brightness in it at all.

He sat down at the table and began once more the task of constructing a handy model steam-engine, but he speedily realised, what he had suspected before, that the instructions were the work of a dangerous madman. What was the good of going on living when gibbering lunatics were allowed to write for weekly papers?

About this time his gloom was deepened by the discovery that a tin labelled mixed biscuits, which he had noticed in Brodie's locker, was empty.

He thought he would go for a stroll. It would be beastly, of course, but not so beastly as sitting in the junior day-room.

It is just here that the tragedy begins to deepen.

Passing out of Seymour's gate he met Brooke, of Appleby's. Brooke wore an earnest, thoughtful expression.

"Hullo, Brooke," said Chapple, "where are you off to?"

It seemed that Brooke was off to the carpenter's shop. Hence the earnest, thoughtful expression. His mind was wrestling with certain pieces of wood which he proposed to fashion into photograph frames. There was always a steady demand in the school for photograph frames, and the gifted were in the habit of turning here and there an honest penny by means of them.

The artist soul is not always unfavourable to a gallery. Brooke said he didn't mind if Chapple came along, only he wasn't to go rotting about or anything. So Chapple went along.

Arrived at the carpenter's shop, Brooke was soon absorbed in his labours. Chapple watched him for a time with the interest of a brother-worker, for had he not tried to construct handy model steam-engines in his day? Indeed, yes. After a while, however, the *rtle* of spectator began to pall. He wanted to *do* something. Wandering round the room he found a chisel, and upon the instant, in direct contravention of the treaty respecting rotting, he sat down and started carving his name on a smooth deal board which looked as if nobody wanted it. The pair worked on in silence, broken only by an occasional hard breath as the toil grew exciting. Chapple's tongue was out and performing mystic evolutions as he carved the letters. He felt inspired.

He was beginning the A when he was brought to earth again by the voice of Brooke.

"You *are* an idiot," said Brooke, complainingly. "That's *my* board, and now you've spoilt it."

Spoilt it! Chapple liked that! Spoilt it, if you please, when he had done a beautiful piece of carving on it!

"Well, it can't be helped now," said Brooke, philosophically. "I suppose it's not your fault you're such an ass. Anyhow, come on now. It's struck eight."

"It's what?" gasped Chapple.

"Struck eight. But it doesn't matter. Appleby never minds one being a bit late for breakfast."

"Oh," said Chapple. "Oh, doesn't he!"

Go into Seymour's at eight sharp any morning and look down the table, and you will see the face of G. M. Chapple—obscured every now and then, perhaps, by a coffee cup or a slice of bread and marmalade. He has not been late for three weeks. The spare room is now occupied by Postlethwaite, of the Upper Fourth, whose place in Milton's dormitory has been taken by Chapple. Milton is the head of the house, and stands alone among the house prefects for the strenuousness of his methods in dealing with his dormitory. Nothing in this world is certain, but it is highly improbable that Chapple will be late again. There are swagger-sticks.

Shields' And The Cricket Cup

The house cricket cup at Wrykyn has found itself on some strange mantelpieces in its time. New talent has a way of cropping up in the house matches. Tail-end men hit up fifties, and bowlers who have never taken a wicket before except at the nets go on fifth change, and dismiss first eleven experts with deliveries that bounce twice and shoot. So that nobody is greatly surprised in the ordinary run of things if the cup does not go to the favourites, or even to the second or third favourites. But one likes to draw the line. And Wrykyn drew it at Shields'. And yet, as we shall proceed to show, Shields' once won the cup, and that, too, in a year when Donaldson's had four first eleven men and Dexter's three.

Shields' occupied a unique position at the School. It was an absolutely inconspicuous house. There were other houses that were slack or wild or both, but the worst of these did something. Shields' never did anything. It never seemed to want to do anything. This may have been due in some degree to Mr. Shields. As the housemaster is, so the house is. He was the most inconspicuous master on the staff. He taught a minute form in the junior school, where earnest infants wrestled with somebody's handy book of easy Latin sentences, and depraved infants threw cunningly compounded ink-balls at one another and the ceiling. After school he would range the countryside with a pickle-bottle in search of polly woggles and other big game, which he subsequently transferred to slides and examined through a microscope till an advanced hour of the night. The curious part of the matter was that his house was never riotous. Perhaps he was looked on as a non-combatant, one whom it would be unfair and unsporting to rag. At any rate, a weird calm reigned over the place; and this spirit seemed to permeate the public lives of the Shieldsites. They said nothing much and they did nothing much and they were very inoffensive. As a rule, one hardly knew they were there.

Into this abode of lotus-eaters came Clephane, a day boy, owing to the departure of his parents for India. Clephane wanted to go to Donaldson's. In fact, he said so. His expressions, indeed, when he found that the whole thing had been settled, and that he was to spend his last term at school at a house which had never turned out so much as a member of the Gym. Six, bordered on the unfilial. It appeared that his father had met Mr. Shields at dinner in the town—a fact to which he seemed to attach a mystic importance. Clephane's criticism of this attitude of mind was of such a nature as to lead his father to address him as Archibald instead of Archie.

However, the thing was done, and Clephane showed his good sense by realising this and turning his energetic mind to the discovery of the best way of making life at Shields' endurable. Fortune favoured him by sending to the house another day boy, one Mansfield. Clephane had not known him intimately before, though they were both members of the second eleven; but at Shields' they instantly formed an alliance. And in due season—or a little later—the house matches began. Henfrey, of Day's, the Wrykyn cricket captain, met Clephane at the nets when the drawing for opponents had been done.

"Just the man I wanted to see," said Henfrey. "I suppose you're captain of Shields' lot, Clephane? Well, you're going to scratch as usual, I suppose?"

For the last five seasons that lamentable house had failed to put a team into the field. "You'd better," said Henfrey, "we haven't overmuch time as it is. That match with Paget's team has thrown us out a lot. We ought to have started the house matches a week ago."

"Scratch!" said Clephane. "Don't you wish we would! My good chap, we're going to get the cup."

"You needn't be a funny ass," said Henfrey in his complaining voice, "we really are awfully pushed. As it is we shall have to settle the opening rounds on the first innings. That's to say, we can only give 'em a day each; if they don't finish, the winner of the first innings wins. You might as well scratch."

"I can't help your troubles. By rotten mismanagement you have got the house-matches crowded up into the last ten days of term, and you come and expect me to sell a fine side like Shields' to get you out of the consequences of your reckless act. My word, Henfrey, you've sunk pretty low. Nice young fellow Henfrey was at one time, but seems to have got among bad companions. Quite changed now. Avoid him as much as I can. Leave me, Henfrey, I would be alone."

"But you can't raise a team."

"Raise a team! Do you happen to know that half the house is *biting* itself with agony because we can't find room for all? Shields gives stump-cricket *soiries* in his study after prep. One every time you hit the ball, two into the bowl of goldfish, and out if you smash the microscope."

"Well," said Henfrey viciously, "if you want to go through the farce of playing one round and making idiots of yourselves, you'll have to wait a bit. You've got a bye in the first round."

Clephane told the news to Mansfield after tea. "I've been and let the house in for a rollicking time," he said, abstracting the copy of Latin verses which his friend was doing, and sitting on them to ensure undivided attention to his words. "Wanting to score off old Henfrey—I have few pleasures—I told him that Shields' was not going to scratch. So we are booked to play in the second round of the housers. We drew a bye for the first. It would be an awful rag if we could do something. We *must* raise a team of some sort. Henfrey would score so if we didn't. Who's there, d'you think, that can play?"

Mansfield considered the question thoughtfully. "They all *play*, I suppose," he said slowly, "if you can call it playing. What I mean to say is, cricket's compulsory here, so I suppose they've all had an innings or two at one time or another in the eightieth game or so. But if you want record-breakers, I shouldn't trust to Shields' too much."

"Not a bit. So long as we put a full team into the field, that's all I care about. I've often wondered what it's like to go in first and bowl unchanged the whole time."

"You'll do that all right," said Mansfield. "I should think Shields' bowling ran to slow grubs, to judge from the look of 'em. You'd better go and see Wilkins about raising the team. As head of the house, he probably considers himself captain of cricket."

Wilkins, however, took a far more modest view of his position. The notion of leading a happy band of cricketers from Shields' into the field had, it seemed, small attractions for him. But he went so far as to get a house list, and help choose a really representative team. And as details about historic teams are always welcome, we may say that the averages ranged from 3.005 to 8.14. This last was Wilkins' own and was, as he would have been the first to admit, substantially helped by a contribution of nineteen in a single innings in the fifth game.

So the team was selected, and Clephane turned out after school next day to give them a little fielding-practice. To his surprise the fielding was not so outrageous as might have been expected. All the simpler catches were held, and one or two of the harder as well. Given this form on the day of their appearance in public, and Henfrey might be disappointed when he came to watch and smile sarcastically. A batting fiasco is not one half so ridiculous as maniac fielding.

In the meantime the first round of the house matches had been played off, and it would be as well to describe at this point the positions of the rival houses and their prospects. In the first place, there were only four teams really in the running for the cup, Day's (headed by the redoubtable Henfrey), Spence's, who had Jackson, that season a head and shoulders above the other batsmen in the first eleven—he had just wound up the school season with an average of 51.3, Donaldson's, and Dexter's. All the other house teams were mainly tail.

Now, in the first round the powerful quartette had been diminished by the fact that Donaldson's had drawn Dexter's, and had lost to them by a couple of wickets.

For the second round Shields' drew Appleby's, a poor team. Space on the Wrykyn field being a consideration, with three house matches to be played off at the same time, Clephane's men fought their first battle on rugged ground in an obscure corner. As the captain of cricket ordered these matters, Henfrey had naturally selected the best bit of turf for Day's *v.* Dexter's. That section of the ground which was sacred to the school second-eleven matches was allotted to Spence's *v.* the School House. The idle public divided its attention between the two big games, and paid no attention to the death struggle in progress at the far end of the field. Whereby it missed a deal of quiet fun.

I say death struggle advisedly. Clephane had won his second-eleven cap as a fast bowler. He had failed to get into the first eleven because he was considered too erratic. Put these two facts together, and you will suspect that dark deeds were wrought on the men of Appleby in that lonely corner of the Wrykyn meadow.

The pitch was not a good one. As a sample of the groundman's art it was sketchy and amateurish; it lacked finish. Clephane won the toss, took a hasty glance at the corrugated turf, and decided to bat first. The wicket was hardly likely to improve with use.

He and Mansfield opened the batting. He stood three feet out of his ground, and smote. The first four balls he took full pitch. The last two, owing to a passion for variety on the part of the bowler, were long hops. At the end of the over Shields' score was twenty-four. Mansfield pursued the same tactics. When the first wicket fell, seventy was on the board. A spirit of martial enthusiasm pervaded the ranks of the house team. Mild youths with spectacles leaped out of their ground like tigers, and snicked fours through the slips. When the innings concluded, blood had been spilt— from an injured finger—but the total was a hundred and two.

Then Clephane walked across to the School shop for a vanilla ice. He said he could get more devil, as it were, into his bowling after a vanilla ice. He had a couple.

When he bowled his first ball it was easy to see that there was truth in the report of the causes of his inclusion in the second eleven and exclusion from the first. The batsman observed somewhat weakly, "Here, I *say!*" and backed towards square leg. The ball soared over the wicket-keep's head and went to the boundary. The bowler grinned pleasantly, and said he was just getting his arm in.

The second ball landed full-pitch on the batsman's right thigh. The third was another full pitch, this time on the top of the middle stump, which it smashed. With profound satisfaction the batsman hobbled to the trees, and sat down. "Let somebody else have a shot," he said kindly.

Appleby's made twenty-eight that innings.

Their defeat by an innings and fifty-three runs they attributed subsequently to the fact that only seven of the team could be induced to go to the wickets in the second venture.

"So you've managed to win a match," grunted Henfrey, "I should like to have been there."

"You might just as well have been," said Clephane, "from what they tell me."

At which Henfrey became abusive, for he had achieved an "egg" that afternoon, and missed a catch; which things soured him, though Day's had polished off Dexter's handsomely.

"Well," he said at length, "you're in the semi-final now, of all weird places. You'd better play Spence's next. When can you play?"

"Henfrey," said Clephane, "I have a bright, open, boyish countenance, but I was not born yesterday. You want to get a dangerous rival out of the way without trouble, so you set Shields' to smash up Spence's. No, Henfrey. I do not intend to be your catspaw. We will draw lots who is to play which. Here comes Jackson. We'll toss odd man out."

And when the coins fell there were two tails and one head; and the head belonged to the coin of Clephane.

"So, you see," he said to Henfrey, "Shields' is in the final. No wonder you wanted us to scratch."

I should like this story to end with a vivid description of a tight finish. Considering that Day's beat Spence's, and consequently met Shields' in the final, that would certainly be the most artistic ending. Henfrey batting—Clephane bowling—one to tie, two to win, one wicket to fall. Up goes the ball! Will the lad catch it!! He fumbles it. It falls. All is over. But look! With a supreme effort—and so on.

The real conclusion was a little sensational in its way, but not nearly so exciting as that.

The match between Day's and Shields' opened in a conventional enough manner. Day's batted first, and made two hundred and fifty. Henfrey carried his bat for seventy-six, and there were some thirties. For Shields' Clephane and Mansfield made their usual first-wicket stand, and the rest brought the total up to ninety-eight. At this point Henfrey introduced a variation on custom. The match was a three days' match. In fact, owing to the speed with which the other games had been played, it could, if necessary, last four days. The follow-on was, therefore, a matter for the discretion of the side which led. Henfrey and his team saw no reason why they should not have another pleasant spell of batting before dismissing their opponents for the second time and acquiring the cup. So in they went again, and made another two hundred and fifty odd, Shields' being left with four hundred and twelve to make to win.

On the morning after Day's second innings, a fag from Day's brought Clephane a message from Henfrey. Henfrey was apparently in bed. He would be glad if Clephane would go and see him in the dinner-hour. The interview lasted fifteen minutes. Then Clephane burst out of the house, and dashed across to Shields' in search of Mansfield.

"I say, *have* you heard?" he shouted.

"What's up?"

"Why, every man in Day's team, bar two kids, is in bed. Ill. Do you mean to say you haven't heard? They thought they'd got that house cup safe, so all the team except the two kids, fags, you know, had a feed in honour of it in Henfrey's study. Some ass went and bought a bad rabbit pie, and now they're laid up. Not badly, but they won't be out for a day or two."

"But what about the match?"

"Oh, that'll go on. I made a point of that. They can play subs."

Mansfield looked thoughtful.

"But I say," he said, "it isn't very sporting, is it? Oughtn't we to wait or something?"

"Sporting! My dear chap, a case like this mustn't be judged by ordinary standards. We can't spoil the giant rag of the century because it isn't quite sporting. Think what it means—Shields' getting the cup! It'll keep the school laughing for terms. What do you want to spoil people's pleasure for?"

"Oh, all right," said Mansfield.

"Besides, think of the moral effect it'll have on the house. It may turn it into the blood house of Wrykyn.

Shields himself may get quite sportive. We mustn't miss the chance."

The news having got about the school, Clephane and Mansfield opened their second innings to the somewhat embarrassed trundling of Masters Royce and Tibbit, of the Junior School, before a substantial and appreciative audience.

Both played carefully at first, but soon getting the measure of the bowling (which was not deep) began to hit out, and runs came quickly. At fifty, Tibbit, understudying Henfrey as captain of the side, summoned to his young friend Todby from short leg, and instructed him to "have a go" at the top end.

It was here that Clephane courteously interfered. Substitutes, he pointed out, were allowed, by the laws of cricket, only to field, not to bowl. He must, therefore, request friend Todby to return to his former sphere of utility, where, he added politely, he was a perfect demon.

"But, blow it," said Master Tibbit, who (alas!) was addicted to the use of strong language, "Royce and I can't bowl the whole blessed time."

"You'll have to, I'm afraid," said Clephane with the kindly air of a doctor soothing a refractory patient. "Of course, you can take a spell at grubs whenever you like."

"Oh, darn!" said Master Tibbit.

Shortly afterwards Clephane made his century.

The match ended late on the following afternoon in a victory for Shields' by nine wickets, and the scene at the School Shop when Royce and Tibbit arrived to drown their sorrows and moisten their dry throats with ginger beer is said by eyewitnesses to have been something quite out of the common run.

The score sheet of the match is also a little unusual. Clephane's three hundred and one (not out) is described in the *Wrykinian* as a "masterly exhibition of sound yet aggressive batting." How Henfrey described it we have never heard.

An International Affair

Part 1

The whole thing may be said to have begun when Mr. Oliver Ring of New York, changing cars, as he called it, at Wrykyn on his way to London, had to wait an hour for his train. He put in that hour by strolling about the town and seeing the sights, which were not numerous. Wrykyn, except on Market Day, was wont to be wrapped in a primaeval calm which very nearly brought tears to the strenuous eyes of the man from Manhattan. He had always been told that England was a slow country, and his visit, now in its third week, had confirmed this opinion: but even in England he had not looked to find such a lotus-eating place as Wrykyn. He looked at the shop windows. They resembled the shop windows of every other country town in England. There was no dash, no initiative about them. They did not leap to the eye and arrest the pedestrian's progress. They ordered these things, thought Mr. Ring, better in the States. And then something seemed to whisper to him that here was the place to set up a branch of Ring's Come-One Come-All Up-to-date Stores. During his stroll he had gathered certain pieces of information. To wit, that Wrykyn was where the county families for ten miles round did their shopping, that the population of the town was larger than would appear at first sight to a casual observer, and, finally, that there was a school of six hundred boys only a mile away. Nothing could be better. Within a month he would take to himself the entire trade of the neighbourhood.

"It's a cinch," murmured Mr. Ring with a glad smile, as he boarded his train, "a lead-pipe cinch."

Everybody who has moved about the world at all knows Ring's Come-one Come-all Up-to-date Stores. The main office is in New York. Broadway, to be exact, on the left as you go down, just before you get to Park Row, where the newspapers come from. There is another office in Chicago. Others in St. Louis, St. Paul, and across the seas in London, Paris, Berlin, and, in short, everywhere. The peculiar advantage about Ring's Stores is that you can get anything you happen to want there, from a motor to a macaroon, and rather cheaper than you could get it anywhere else. England had up to the present been ill-supplied with these handy paradises, the one in Piccadilly being the only extant specimen. But now Mr. Ring in person had crossed the Atlantic on a tour of inspection, and things were shortly to be so brisk that you would be able to hear them whizz.

So an army of workmen invaded Wrykyn. A trio of decrepit houses in the High Street were pulled down with a run, and from the ruins there began to rise like a Phoenix the striking building which was to be the

Wrykyn Branch of Ring's Come-one Come-all Up-to-date Stores.

The sensation among the tradesmen caused by the invasion was, as may be imagined, immense and painful. The thing was a public disaster. It resembled the advent of a fox in a fowl-run. For years the tradesmen of Wrykyn had jogged along in their comfortable way, each making his little profits, with no thought of competition or modern hustle. And now the enemy was at their doors. Many were the gloomy looks cast at the gaudy building as it grew like a mushroom. It was finished with incredible speed, and then advertisements began to flood the local papers. A special sheaf of bills was despatched to the school.

Dunstable got hold of one, and read it with interest. Then he went in search of his friend Linton to find out what he thought of it.

Linton was at work in the laboratory. He was an enthusiastic, but unskilful, chemist. The only thing he could do with any real certainty was to make oxygen. But he had ambitions beyond that feat, and was continually experimenting in a reckless way which made the chemistry master look wan and uneasy. He was bending over a complicated mixture of tubes, acids, and Bunsen burners when Dunstable found him. It was after school, so that the laboratory was empty, but for them.

"Don't mind me," said Dunstable, taking a seat on the table.

"Look out, man, don't jog. Sit tight, and I'll broaden your mind for you. I take this bit of litmus paper, and dip it into this bilge, and if I've done it right, it'll turn blue."

"Then I bet it doesn't," said Dunstable.

The paper turned red.

"Hades," said Linton calmly. "Well, I'm not going to sweat at it any more. Let's go down to Cook's."

Cook's is the one school institution which nobody forgets who has been to Wrykyn. It is a little confectioner's shop in the High Street. Its exterior is somewhat forbidding, and the uninitiated would probably shudder and pass on, wondering how on earth such a place could find a public daring enough to support it by eating its wares. But the school went there in flocks. Tea at Cook's was the alternative to a study tea. There was a large room at the back of the shop, and here oceans of hot tea and tons of toast were consumed. The staff of Cook's consisted of Mr. Cook, late sergeant in a line regiment, six foot three, disposition amiable, left leg cut off above the knee by a spirited Fuzzy in the last Soudan war; Mrs. Cook, wife of the above, disposition similar, and possessing the useful gift of being able to listen to five people at one and the same time; and an invisible menial, or menials, who made toast in some nether region at a perfectly dizzy rate of speed. Such was Cook's.

"Talking of Cook's," said Dunstable, producing his pamphlet, "have you seen this? It'll be a bit of a knock-out for them, I should think."

Linton took the paper, and began to read. Dunstable roamed curiously about the laboratory, examining things.

"What are these little crystal sort of bits of stuff?" he asked, coming to a standstill before a large jar and opening it. "They look good to eat. Shall I try one?"

"Don't you be an idiot," said the expert, looking up. "What have you got hold of? Great Scott, no, don't eat that stuff."

"Why not? Is it poison?"

"No. But it would make you sick as a cat. It's Sal Ammoniac."

"Sal how much?"

"Ammoniac. You'd be awfully bad."

"All right, then, I won't. Well, what do you think of that thing? It'll be rough on Cook's, won't it? You see they advertise a special 'public-school' tea, as they call it. It sounds jolly good. I don't know what buckwheat cakes are, but they ought to be decent. I suppose now everybody'll chuck Cook's and go there. It's a beastly shame, considering that Cook's has been a sort of school shop so long. And they really depend on the school. At least, one never sees anybody else going there. Well, I shall stick to Cook's. I don't want any of your beastly Yankee invaders. Support home industries.

Be a patriot. The band then played God Save the King, and the meeting dispersed. But, seriously, man, I am rather sick about this. The Cooks are such awfully good sorts, and this is bound to make them lose a tremendous lot. The school's simply crawling with chaps who'd do anything to get a good tea cheaper than they're getting now. They'll simply scrum in to this new place."

"Well, I don't see what we can do," said Linton, "except keep on going to Cook's ourselves. Let's be going now, by the way. We'll get as many chaps as we can to promise to stick to them. But we can't prevent the rest going where they like. Come on."

The atmosphere at Cook's that evening was heavily charged with gloom. ExSergeant Cook, usually a treasury of jest and anecdote, was silent and thoughtful. Mrs. Cook bustled about with her customary vigour, but she too was disinclined for conversation. The place was ominously empty. A quartette of school house juniors in one corner and a solitary prefect from Donaldson's completed the sum of the customers. Nobody seemed to want to talk a great deal. There was something in the air which

said as plain as whisper in the ear,

"The place is haunted."

and so it was. Haunted by the spectre of that hideous, new, glaring red-brick building down the street, which had opened its doors to the public on the previous afternoon.

"Look there," said Dunstable, as they came out. He pointed along the street. The doors of the new establishment were congested. A crowd, made up of members of various houses, was pushing to get past another crowd which was trying to get out. The "public-school tea at one shilling" appeared to have proved attractive.

"Look at 'em," said Dunstable. "Sordid beasts! All they care about is filling themselves. There goes that man Merrett. Rand-Brown with him. Here come four more. Come on. It makes me sick."

"I wish it would make *them* sick," said Linton.

"Perhaps it will.... By George!"

He started.

"What's up?" said Linton.

"Oh, nothing. I was only thinking of something."

They walked on without further conversation. Dunstable's brain was working fast. He had an idea, and was busy developing it.

The manager of the Wrykyn Branch of Ring's Come-one Come-all Stores stood at the entrance to his shop on the following afternoon spitting with energy and precision on to the pavement—he was a free-born American citizen—and eyeing the High Street as a monarch might gaze at his kingdom. He had just completed a highly satisfactory report to headquarters, and was feeling contented with the universe, and the way in which it was managed. Even in the short time since the opening of the store he had managed to wake up the sluggish Britishers as if they had had an electric shock.

"We," he observed epigrammatically to a passing cat, which had stopped on its way to look at him, "are it."

As he spoke he perceived a youth coming towards him down the street. He wore a cap of divers colours, from which the manager argued that he belonged to the school. Evidently a devotee of the advertised "public-school" shillingsworth, and one who, as urged by the small bills, had come early to avoid the rush. "Step right in, mister," he said, moving aside from the doorway. "And what can I do for *you*?"

"Are you the manager of this place?" asked Dunstable—for the youth was that strategist, and no other.

"On the bull's eye first time," replied the manager with easy courtesy. "Will you take a cigar or a cocoa-nut?"

"Can I have a bit of a talk with you, if you aren't busy?"

"Sure. Step right in."

"Now, sir," said the manager, "what's *your* little trouble?"

"It's about this public school tea business," said Dunstable. "It's rather a shame, you see. Before you came bargeing in, everybody used to go to Cook's."

"And now," interrupted the manager, "they come to us. Correct, sir. We *are* the main stem. And why not?"

"Cook's such a good sort."

"I should like to know him," said the manager politely.

"You see," said Dunstable, "it doesn't so much matter about the other things you sell; but Cook's simply relies on giving fellows tea in the afternoon——"

"One moment, sir," said the man from the States. "Let me remind you of a little rule which will be useful to you when you butt into the big, cold world. That is, never let sentiment interfere with business. See? Either Ring's Stores or your friend has got to be on top, and, if I know anything, it's going to be We. We! And I'm afraid that's all I can do for you, unless you've that hungry feeling, and want to sample our public-school tea at twenty-five cents."

"No, thanks," said Dunstable. "Here come some chaps, though, who look as if they might."

He stepped aside as half a dozen School House juniors raced up.

"For one day only," said the manager to Dunstable, "you may partake free, if you care to. You have man's most priceless possession, Cool Cheek. And Cool Cheek, when recognised, should not go unrewarded. Step in."

"No thanks," said Dunstable. "You'll find me at Cook's if you want me."

"Kindness," said he to himself, as Mrs. Cook served him in the depressed way which had now become habitual with her, "kindness having failed, we must try severity."

Part 2

Those who knew and liked Dunstable were both pained and disgusted at his behaviour during the ensuing three days. He suddenly exhibited a weird fondness for some of Wrykyn's least deserving inmates. He walked over to school with Merrett, of Seymour's, and Ruthven, of Donaldson's, both notorious outsiders. When Linton wanted him to come and play fives after school, he declined on the ground that he was teaing with Chadwick, of Appleby's. Now in the matter of absolute outsiderishness Chadwick, of Appleby's, was to Merrett, of Seymour's, as captain is to subaltern. Linton was horrified, and said so.

"What do you want to do it for?" he asked. "What's the point of it? You can't like those chaps."

"Awfully good sorts when you get to know them," said Dunstable.

"You've been some time finding it out."

"I know. Chadwick's an acquired taste. By the way, I'm giving a tea on Thursday. Will you come?"

"Who's going to be there?" inquired Linton warily.

"Well, Chadwick for one; and Merrett and Ruthven and three other chaps."

"Then," said Linton with some warmth, "I think you'll have to do without me. I believe you're mad."

And he went off in disgust to the fives-courts.

When on the following Thursday Dunstable walked into Ring's Stores with his five guests, and demanded six public-school teas, the manager was perhaps justified in allowing a triumphant smile to wander across his face. It was a signal victory for him. "No free list to-day, sir," he said. "Entirely suspended."

"Never mind," said Dunstable, "I'm good for six shillings."

"Free list?" said Merrett, as the manager retired, "I didn't know there was one."

"There isn't. Only he and I palled up so much the other day that he offered me a tea for nothing."

"Didn't you take it?"

"No. I went to Cook's."

"Rotten hole, Cook's. I'm never going there again," said Chadwick. "You take my tip, Dun, old chap, and come here."

"Dun, old chap," smiled amiably.

"I don't know," he said, looking up from the tea-pot, into which he had been pouring water; "you can be certain of the food at Cook's."

"What do you mean? So you can here."

"Oh," said Dunstable, "I didn't know. I've never had tea here before. But I've often heard that American food upsets one sometimes."

By this time, the tea having stood long enough, he poured out, and the meal began.

Merrett and his friends were hearty feeders, and conversation languished for some time. Then Chadwick leaned back in his chair, and breathed heavily.

"You couldn't get stuff like that at Cook's," he said.

"I suppose it is a bit different," said Dunstable. "Have any of you ... noticed something queer...?"

Merrett stared at Ruthven. Ruthven stared at Merrett.

"I...." said Merrett.

"D'you know...." said Ruthven.

Chadwick's face was a delicate green.

"I believe," said Dunstable, "the stuff ... was ... poisoned. I...."

"Drink this," said the school doctor, briskly, bending over Dunstable's bed with a medicine-glass in his hand, "and be ashamed of yourself. The fact is you've over-eaten yourself. Nothing more and nothing less. Why can't you boys be content to feed moderately?"

"I don't think I ate much, sir," protested Dunstable. "It must have been what I ate. I went to that new American place."

"So *you* went there, too? Why, I've just come from attending a bilious boy in Mr. Seymour's house. He said he had been at the American place, too."

"Was that Merrett, sir? He was one of the party. We were all bad. We can't all have eaten too much."

The doctor looked thoughtful.

"H'm. Curious. Very curious. Do you remember what you had?"

"I had some things the man called buckwheat cakes, with some stuff he said was maple syrup."

"Bah. American trash." The doctor was a staunch Briton, conservative in his views both on politics and on food. "Why can't you boys eat good English food? I must tell the headmaster of this. I haven't time to look after the school if all the boys are going to poison themselves. You lie still and try to go to sleep, and you'll be right enough in no time."

But Dunstable did not go to sleep. He stayed awake to interview Linton, who came to pay him a visit.

"Well," said Linton, looking down at the sufferer with an expression that was a delicate blend of pity and contempt, "you've made a nice sort of ass of yourself, haven't you! I don't know if it's any consolation to you, but Merrett's just as bad as you are. And I hear the others are, too. So now you see what comes of going to Ring's instead of Cook's."

"And now," said Dunstable, "if you've quite finished, you can listen to me for a bit...."

"So now you know," he concluded.

Linton's face beamed with astonishment and admiration.

"Well, I'm hanged," he said. "You're a marvel. But how did you know it wouldn't poison you?"

"I relied on you. You said it wasn't poison when I asked you in the lab. My faith in you is touching."

"But why did you take any yourself?"

"Sort of idea of diverting suspicion. But the thing isn't finished yet. Listen."

Linton left the dormitory five minutes later with a look of a young disciple engaged on some holy mission.

Part 3

"You think the food is unwholesome, then?" said the headmaster after dinner that night.

"Unwholesome!" said the school doctor. "It must be deadly. It must be positively lethal. Here we have six ordinary, strong, healthy boys struck down at one fell swoop as if there were a pestilence raging. Why——"

"One moment," said the headmaster. "Come in."

A small figure appeared in the doorway.

"Please, sir," said the figure in the strained voice of one speaking a "piece" which he has committed to memory. "Mr. Seymour says please would you mind letting the doctor come to his house at once because Linton is ill."

"What!" exclaimed the doctor. "What's the matter with him?"

"Please, sir, I believe it's buckwheat cakes."

"What! And here's another of them!"

A second small figure had appeared in the doorway.

"Sir, please, sir," said the newcomer, "Mr. Bradfield says may the doctor——"

"And what boy is it *this* time?"

"Please, sir, it's Brown. He went to Ring's Stores——"

The headmaster rose.

"Perhaps you had better go at once, Oakes," he said. "This is becoming serious. That place is a positive menace to the community. I shall put it out of bounds tomorrow morning."

And when Dunstable and Linton, pale but cheerful, made their way—slowly, as befitted convalescents—to Cook's two days afterwards, they had to sit on the counter. All the other seats were occupied.

The Guardian

In his Sunday suit (with ten shillings in specie in the right-hand trouser pocket) and a brand-new bowler hat, the youngest of the Shearnes, Thomas Beauchamp Algernon, was being launched by the combined strength of the family on his public-school career. It was a solemn moment. The landscape was dotted with relatives—here a small sister, awed by the occasion into refraining from insult; there an aunt, vaguely admonitory. "Well, Tom," said Mr. Shearne, "you'll soon be off now. You're sure to like Eckleton. Remember to cultivate your bowling. Everyone can bat nowadays. And play forward, not outside. The outsides get most of the fun, certainly, but then if you're a forward, you've got eight chances of getting into a team."

"All right, father."

"Oh, and work hard." This by way of an afterthought.

"All right, father."

"And, Tom," said Mrs. Shearne, "you are sure to be comfortable at school, because I asked Mrs. Davy to write to her sister, Mrs. Spencer, who has a son at

Eckleton, and tell her to tell him to look after you when you get there. He is in Mr. Dencroft's house, which is next door to Mr. Blackburn's, so you will be quite close to one another. Mind you write directly you get there."

"All right, mother."

"And look here, Tom." His eldest brother stepped to the front and spoke earnestly. "Look here, don't you forget what I've been telling you?"

"All right."

"You'll be right enough if you don't go sticking on side. Don't forget that, however much of a blood you may have been at that rotten little private school of yours, you're not one at Eckleton."

"All right."

"You look clean, which is the great thing. There's nothing much wrong with you except cheek. You've got enough of that to float a ship. Keep it under."

"All right. Keep your hair on."

"There you go," said the expert, with gloomy triumph. "If you say that sort of thing at Eckleton, you'll get jolly well sat on, by Jove!"

"Bai Jove, old chap!" murmured the younger brother, "we're devils in the Forty-twoth!"

The other, whose chief sorrow in life was that he could not get the smaller members of the family to look with proper awe on the fact that he had just passed into Sandhurst, gazed wistfully at the speaker, but, realising that there was a locked door between them, tried no active measures.

"Well, anyhow," he said, "you'll soon get it knocked out of you, that's one comfort. Look here, if you do get scrapping with anybody, don't forget all I've taught you. And I should go on boxing there if I were you, so as to go down to Aldershot some day. You ought to make a fairly decent featherweight if you practise."

"All right."

"Let's know when Eckleton's playing Haileybury, and I'll come and look you up. I want to see that match."

"All right."

"Good-bye."

"Good-bye, Tom."

"Good-bye, Tom, dear."

Chorus of aunts and other supers: "Goodbye, Tom."

Tom (comprehensively): "G'bye."

The train left the station.

Kennedy, the head of Dencroft's, said that when he wanted his study turned into a beastly furnace, he would take care to let Spencer know. He pointed out that just because it was his habit to warm the study during the winter months, there was no reason why

Spencer should light the gas-stove on an afternoon in the summer term when the thermometer was in the eighties. Spencer thought he might want some muffins cooked for tea, did he? Kennedy earnestly advised Spencer to give up thinking, as Nature had not equipped him for the strain. Thinking necessitated mental effort, and Spencer, in Kennedy's opinion, had no mind, but rubbed along on a cheap substitute of mud and putty.

More chatty remarks were exchanged, and then Spencer tore himself away from the pleasant interview, and went downstairs to the junior study, where he remarked to his friend Phipps that Life was getting a bit thick.

"What's up now?" inquired Phipps.

"Everything. We've just had a week of term, and I've been in extra once already for doing practically nothing, and I've got a hundred lines, and Kennedy's been slanging me for lighting the stove. How was I to know he didn't want it lit? Wish I was fagging for somebody else."

"All the while you're jawing," said Phipps, "there's a letter for you on the mantelpiece, staring at you?"

"So there is. Hullo!"

"What's up? Hullo! is that a postal order? How much for?"

"Five bob. I say, who's Shearne?"

"New kid in Blackburn's. Why?"

"Great Scott! I remember now. They told me to look after him. I haven't seen him yet. And listen to this: 'Mrs. Shearne has sent me the enclosed to give to you. Her son writes to say that he is very happy and getting on very well, so she is sure you must have been looking after him.' Why, I don't know the kid by sight. I clean forgot all about him."

"Well, you'd better go and see him now, just to say you've done it."

Spencer perpended.

"Beastly nuisance having a new kid hanging on to you. He's probably a frightful rotter."

"Well, anyway, you ought to," said Phipps, who possessed the *scenario* of a conscience.

"I can't."

"All right, don't, then. But you ought to send back that postal order."

"Look here, Phipps," said Spencer plaintively, "you needn't be an idiot, you know."

And the trivial matter of Thomas B. A. Shearne was shelved.

Thomas, as he had stated in his letter to his mother, was exceedingly happy at Eckleton, and getting on very nicely indeed. It is true that there had been one or two small unpleasantnesses at first, but those were over now, and he had settled down completely. The little troubles alluded to above had begun on his second day at Blackburn's. Thomas, as the reader may have gathered from his glimpse of him at the station, was not a diffident youth. He was quite prepared for anything Fate might have up its sleeve for him, and he entered the junior day-room at Blackburn's ready for emergencies. On the first day nothing happened. One or two people asked him his name, but none inquired what his father was—a question which, he had understood from books of school life, was invariably put to the new boy. He was thus prevented from replying "coolly, with his eyes fixed on his questioner's": "A gentleman. What's yours?" and this, of course, had been a disappointment. But he reconciled himself to it, and on the whole enjoyed his first day at Eckleton.

On the second there occurred an Episode.

Thomas had inherited from his mother a pleasant, rather meek cast of countenance. He had pink cheeks and golden hair—almost indecently golden in one who was not a choirboy.

Now, if you are going to look like a Ministering Child or a Little Willie, the Sunbeam of the Home, when you go to a public school, you must take the consequences. As Thomas sat by the window of the junior day-room reading a magazine, and deeply interested in it, there fell upon his face such a rapt, angelic expression that the sight of it, silhouetted against the window, roused Master P. Burge, his fellow-Blackburnite, as it had been a trumpet-blast. To seize a

Bradley Arnold's Latin Prose Exercises and hurl it across the room was with Master Burge the work of a moment. It struck Thomas on the ear. He jumped, and turned some shades pinker. Then he put down his magazine, picked up the Bradley Arnold, and sat on it. After which he resumed his magazine.

The acute interest of the junior day-room, always fond of a break in the monotony of things, induced Burge to go further into the matter.

"You with the face!" said Burge rudely.

Thomas looked up.

"What the dickens are you going with my book? Pass it back!"

"Oh, is this yours?" said Thomas. "Here you are."

He walked towards him, carrying the book. At two yards range he fired it in. It hit Burge with some force in the waistcoat, and there was a pause while he collected his wind.

Then the thing may be said to have begun.

Yes, said Burge, interrogated on the point five minutes later, he *had* had enough.

"Good," said Thomas pleasantly. "Want a handkerchief?"

That evening he wrote to his mother and, thanking her for kind inquiries, stated that he was not being bullied. He added, also in answer to inquiries, that he had not been tossed in a blanket, and that—so far—no

Hulking Senior (with scowl) had let him down from the dormitory window after midnight by a sheet, in order that he might procure gin from the local public-house. As far as he could gather, the seniors were mostly teetotallers. Yes, he had seen Spencer several times. He did not add that he had seen him from a distance.

"I'm so glad I asked Mrs. Davy to get her nephew to look after Tom," said Mrs. Shearne, concluding the reading of the epistle at breakfast. "It makes such a difference to a new boy having somebody to protect him at first."

"Only drawback is," said his eldest brother gloomily—"won't get cheek knocked out of him. Tom's kid wh'ought get'sheadsmacked reg'ly. Be no holding him."

And he helped himself to marmalade, of which delicacy his mouth was full, with a sort of magnificent despondency.

By the end of the first fortnight of his school career, Thomas Beauchamp Algernon had overcome all the little ruggednesses which relieve the path of the new boy from monotony. He had been taken in by a primaeval "sell" which the junior day-room invariably sprang on the new-comer. But as he had sat on the head of the engineer of the same for the space of ten minutes, despite the latter's complaints of pain and forecasts of what he would do when he got up, the laugh had not been completely against him. He had received the honourable distinction of extra lesson for ragging in French. He had been "touched up" by the prefect of his dormitory for creating a disturbance in the small hours. In fact, he had gone through all the usual preliminaries, and become a full-blown Eckletonian.

His letters home were so cheerful at this point that a second postal order relieved the dwindling fortune of Spencer. And it was this, coupled with the remonstrances of Phipps, that induced the Dencroftian to break through his icy reserve.

"Look here, Spencer," said Phipps, his conscience thoroughly stirred by this second windfall, "it's all rot. You must either send back that postal order, or go and see the chap. Besides, he's quite a decent kid. We're in the same game at cricket. He's rather a good bowler. I'm getting to know him quite well. I've got a jolly sight more right to those postal orders than you have."

"But he's an awful ass to look at," pleaded Spencer.

"What's wrong with him? Doesn't look nearly such a goat as you," said Phipps, with the refreshing directness of youth.

"He's got yellow hair," argued Spencer.

"Why shouldn't he have?"

"He looks like a sort of young Sunday-school kid."

"Well, he jolly well isn't, then, because I happen to know that he's had scraps with some of the fellows in his house, and simply mopped them."

"Well, all right, then," said Spencer reluctantly.

The historic meeting took place outside the school shop at the quarter to eleven interval next morning. Thomas was leaning against the wall, eating a bun. Spencer approached him with half a jam sandwich in his hand. There was an awkward pause.

"Hullo!" said Spencer at last.

"Hullo!" said Thomas.

Spencer finished his sandwich and brushed the crumbs off his trousers. Thomas continued operations on the bun with the concentrated expression of a lunching python.

"I believe your people know my people," said Spencer.

"We have some awfully swell friends," said Thomas. Spencer chewed this thoughtfully awhile.

"Beastly cheek," he said at last.

"Sorry," said Thomas, not looking it.

Spencer produced a bag of gelatines.

"Have one?" he asked.

"What's wrong with 'em?"

"All right, don't."

He selected a gelatine and consumed it.

"Ever had your head smacked?" he inquired courteously.

A slightly strained look came into Thomas's blue eyes.

"Not often," he replied politely. "Why?"

"Oh, I don't know," said Spencer. "I was only wondering."

"Oh?"

"Look here," said Spencer, "my mater told me to look after you."

"Well, you can look after me now if you want to, because I'm going."

And Thomas dissolved the meeting by walking off in the direction of the junior block.

"That kid," said Spencer to his immortal soul, "wants his head smacked, badly."

At lunch Phipps had questions to ask.

"Saw you talking to Shearne in the interval," he said. "What were you talking about?"

"Oh, nothing in particular."

"What did you think of him?"

"Little idiot."

"Ask him to tea this afternoon?"

"No."

"You must. Dash it all, you must do something for him. You've had ten bob out of his people."

Spencer made no reply.

Going to the school shop that afternoon, he found Thomas seated there with Phipps, behind a pot of tea. As a rule, he and Phipps tea'd together, and he resented this desertion.

"Come on," said Phipps. "We were waiting for you."

"Pining away," added Thomas unnecessarily.

Spencer frowned austerely.

"Come and look after me," urged Thomas.

Spencer sat down in silence. For a minute no sound could be heard but the champing of Thomas's jaws as he dealt with a slab of gingerbread.

"Buck up," said Phipps uneasily.

"Give me," said Thomas, "just one loving look."

Spencer ignored the request. The silence became tense once more.

"Coming to the house net, Phipps?" asked Spencer.

"We were going to the baths. Why don't you come?"

"All right," said Spencer.

Doctors tell us that we should allow one hour to elapse between taking food and bathing, but the rule was not rigidly adhered to at Eckleton. The three proceeded straight from the tea-table to the baths.

The place was rather empty when they arrived. It was a little earlier than the majority of Eckletonians bathed. The bath filled up as lock-up drew near. With the exception of a couple of infants splashing about in the shallow end, and a stout youth who dived in from the spring-board, scrambled out, and dived in again, each time flatter than the last, they had the place to themselves.

"What's it like, Gorrick," inquired Phipps of the stout youth, who had just appeared above the surface again, blowing like a whale. The question was rendered necessary by the fact that many years before the boiler at the Eckleton baths had burst, and had never been repaired, with the consequence that the temperature of the water was apt to vary. That is to say, most days it was colder than others.

"Simply boiling," said the man of weight, climbing out. "I say, did I go in all right then?"

"Not bad," said Phipps.

"Bit flat," added Thomas critically.

Gorrick blinked severely at the speaker. A head-waiter at a fashionable restaurant is cordial in his manner compared with a boy who has been at a public school a year, when addressed familiarly by a new boy. After reflecting on the outrage for a moment, he dived in again.

"Worse than ever," said Truthful Thomas.

"Look here!" said Gorrick.

"Oh, come *on*!" exclaimed Phipps, and led Thomas away.

"That kid," said Gorrick to Spencer, "wants his head smacked, badly."

"That's just what I say," agreed Spencer, with the eagerness of a great mind which has found another that thinks alike with itself.

Spencer was the first of the trio ready to enter the water. His movements were wary and deliberate. There was nothing of the professional diver about Spencer. First he stood on the edge and rubbed his arms, regarding the green water beneath with suspicion and dislike. Then, crouching down, he inserted three toes of his left foot, drew them back sharply, and said "Oo!" Then he stood up again. His next move was to slap his chest and dance a few steps, after which he put his right foot into the water, again remarked "Oo!" and resumed Position I.

"Thought you said it was warm," he shouted to Gorrick.

"So it is; hot as anything. Come on in."

And Spencer came on in. Not because he wanted to—for, by rights, there were some twelve more movements to be gone through before he should finally creep in at the shallow end—but because a cold hand, placed suddenly on the small of his back, urged him forward. Down he went, with the water fizzing and bubbling all over and all round him. He swallowed a good deal of it, but there was still plenty left; and what there was was colder than one would have believed possible.

He came to the surface after what seemed to him a quarter of an hour, and struck out for the side. When he got out, Phipps and Thomas had just got in. Gorrick was standing at the end of the cocoanut matting which formed a pathway to the spring-board. Gorrick was blue, but determined.

"I say! Did I go in all right then?" inquired Gorrick.

"How the dickens do I know?" said Spencer, stung to fresh wrath by the inanity of the question.

"Spencer did," said Thomas, appearing in the water below them and holding on to the rail.

"Look here!" cried Spencer; "did you shove me in then?"

"Me! Shove!" Thomas's voice expressed horror and pain. "Why, you dived in. Jolly good one, too. Reminded me of the diving elephants at the Hippodrome."

And he swam off.

"That kid," said Gorrick, gazing after him, "wants his head smacked."

"Badly," agreed Spencer. "Look here! did he shove me in? Did you see him?"

"I was doing my dive. But it must have been him. Phipps never rags in the bath."

Spencer grunted—an expressive grunt—and, creeping down the steps, entered the water again.

It was Spencer's ambition to swim ten lengths of the bath. He was not a young Channel swimmer, and ten lengths represented a very respectable distance to him. He proceeded now to attempt to lower his record. It was not often that he got the bath so much to himself. Usually, there was barely standing-room in the water, and long-distance swimming was impossible. But now, with a clear field, he should, he thought, be able to complete the desired distance.

He was beginning the fifth length before interruption came. Just as he reached halfway, a reproachful voice at his side said: "Oh, Percy, you'll tire yourself!" and a hand on the top of his head propelled him firmly towards the bottom.

Every schoolboy, as Honble. Macaulay would have put it, knows the sensation of being ducked. It is always unpleasant—sometimes more, sometimes less. The present case belonged to the former class. There was just room inside Spencer for another half-pint of water. He swallowed it. When he came to the surface, he swam to the side without a word and climbed out. It was the last straw. Honour could now be satisfied only with gore.

He hung about outside the baths till Phipps and Thomas appeared, then, with a steadfast expression on his face, he walked up to the latter and kicked him.

Thomas seemed surprised, but not alarmed. His eyes grew a little rounder, and the pink on his cheeks deepened. He looked like a choir-boy in a bad temper.

"Hullo! What's up, you ass, Spencer?" inquired Phipps.

Spencer said nothing.

"Where shall we go?" asked Thomas.

"Oh, chuck it!" said Phipps the peacemaker.

Spencer and Thomas were eyeing each other warily.

"You chaps aren't going to fight?" said Phipps.

The notion seemed to distress him.

"Unless he cares to take a kicking," said Spencer suavely.

"Not to-day, I think, thanks," replied Thomas without heat.

"Then, look here!" said Phipps briskly, "I know a ripping little place just off the Lelby Road. It isn't five minutes' walk, and there's no chance of being booked there. Rot if someone was to come and stop it half-way through. It's in a field; thick hedges. No one can see. And I tell you what—I'll keep time. I've got a watch. Two minute rounds, and half-a-minute in between, and I'm the referee; so, if anybody fouls the other chap, I'll stop the fight. See? Come on!"

Of the details of that conflict we have no very clear record. Phipps is enthusiastic, but vague. He speaks in eulogistic terms of a "corker" which Spencer brought off in the second round, and, again, of a "tremendous biff" which Thomas appears to have consummated in the fourth. But of the more subtle points of the fighting he is content merely to state comprehensively that they were "top-hole." As to the result, it would seem that, in the capacity of referee, he declared the affair a draw at the end of the seventh round; and, later, in his capacity of second to both parties, helped his principals home by back and secret ways, one on each arm.

The next items to which the chronicler would call the attention of the reader are two letters.

The first was from Mrs. Shearne to Spencer, and ran as follows—

My Dear Spencer,—I am writing to you direct, instead of through your aunt, because I want to thank you so much for looking after my boy so well. I know what a hard time a new boy has at a public school if he has got nobody to take care of him at first. I heard from Tom this morning. He seems so happy, and so fond of you. He says you are "an awfully decent chap" and "the only chap who has stood up to him at all." I suppose he means "for him." I hope you will come and spend part of your holidays with us. ("Catch me!" said Spencer.)

Yours sincerely,

Isabel Shearne

P.S.—I hope you will manage to buy something nice with

the enclosed.

The enclosed was yet another postal order for five shillings. As somebody wisely observed, a woman's P.S. is always the most important part of her letter.

"That kid," murmured Spencer between swollen lips, "has got cheek enough for eighteen! 'Awfully decent chap!'"

He proceeded to compose a letter in reply, and for dignity combined with lucidity it may stand as a model to young writers.

5 College Grounds,

Eckleton.

Mr. C. F. Spencer begs to present his compliments to Mrs. Shearne,and returns the postal order, because he doesn't see why he should have it. He notes your remarks re my being a decent chap in your favour of the 13th prox., but cannot see where it quite comes in, as the only thing I've done to Mrs. Shearne's son is to fight seven rounds with him in a field, W. G. Phipps refereeing. It was a draw. I got a black eye and rather a whack in the mouth, but gave him beans also, particularly in the wind, which I learned to do from reading "Rodney Stone"—the bit where Bob Whittaker beats the Eyetalian Gondoleery Cove. Hoping that this will be taken in the spirit which is meant,

I remain

Yours sincerely,

C. F. Spencer

One enclosure.

He sent this off after prep., and retired to bed full of spiritual pride.

On the following morning, going to the shop during the interval, he came upon Thomas negotiating a hot bun.

"Hullo!" said Thomas.

As was generally the case after he had had a fair and spirited turn-out with a fellow human being, Thomas had begun to feel that he loved his late adversary as a brother. A wholesome respect, which had hitherto been wanting, formed part of his opinion of him.

"Hullo!" said Spencer, pausing.

"I say," said Thomas.

"What's up?"

"I say, I don't believe we shook hands, did we?"

"I don't remember doing it."

They shook hands. Spencer began to feel that there were points about Thomas, after all.

"I say," said Thomas.

"Hullo?"

"I'm sorry about in the bath, you know. I didn't know you minded being ducked."

"Oh, all right!" said Spencer awkwardly.

Eight bars rest.

"I say," said Thomas.

"Hullo!"

"Doing anything this afternoon?"

"Nothing special, Why?"

"Come and have tea?"

"All right. Thanks."

"I'll wait for you outside the house."

"All right."

It was just here that Spencer regretted that he had sent back that five-shilling postal order. Five good shillings.

Simply chucked away.

Oh, Life, Life!

But they were not, after all. On his plate at breakfast next day Spencer found a letter. This was the letter—

Messrs. J. K. Shearne (father of T. B. A. Shearne) and P. W. Shearne (brother of same) beg to acknowledge receipt of Mr. C. F. Spencer's esteemed communication of yesterday's date, and in reply desire to inform Mr. Spencer of their hearty approval of his attentions to Mr. T. B. A. Shearne's wind. It is their opinion that the above, a nice boy but inclined to cheek, badly needs treatment on these lines occasionally. They therefore beg to return the postal order, together with another for a like sum, and trust that this will meet with Mr. Spencer's approval.

(Signed) J. K. Shearne,

P. W. Shearne.

Two enclosures.

"Of course, what's up really," said Spencer to himself, after reading this, "is that the whole family's jolly well cracked."

His eye fell on the postal orders.

"Still——!" he said.

That evening he entertained Phipps and Thomas B. A. Shearne lavishly at tea.

A Corner In Lines

Of all the useless and irritating things in this world, lines are probably the most useless and the most irritating. In fact, I only know of two people who ever got any good out of them. Dunstable, of Day's, was one, Linton, of Seymour's, the other. For a portion of one winter term they flourished on lines. The more there were set, the better they liked it. They would have been disappointed if masters had given up the habit of doling them out.

Dunstable was a youth of ideas. He saw far more possibilities in the routine of life at Locksley than did the majority of his contemporaries, and every now and then he made use of these possibilities in a way that caused a considerable sensation in the school.

In the ordinary way of school work, however, he was not particularly brilliant, and suffered in consequence. His chief foe was his form-master, Mr. Langridge. The feud between them had begun on Dunstable's arrival in the form two terms before, and had continued ever since. The balance of points lay with the master. The staff has ways of scoring which the school has not. This story really begins with the last day but one of the summer term. It happened that Dunstable's people were going to make their annual migration to Scotland on that day, and the Headmaster, approached on the subject both by letter and in person, saw no reason why—the examinations being over—Dunstable should not leave Locksley a day before the end of term.

He called Dunstable to his study one night after preparation.

"Your father has written to me, Dunstable," he said, "to ask that you may be allowed to go home on Wednesday instead of Thursday. I think that, under the special circumstances, there will be no objection to this. You had better see that the matron packs your boxes."

"Yes, sir," said Dunstable. "Good business," he added to himself, as he left the room.

When he got back to his own den, he began to ponder over the matter, to see if something could not be made out of it. That was Dunstable's way. He never let anything drop until he had made certain that he had exhausted all its possibilities.

Just before he went to bed he had evolved a neat little scheme for scoring off Mr. Langridge. The knowledge of his plans was confined to himself and the Headmaster. His dorm-master would imagine that he was going to stay on till the last day of term. Therefore, if he misbehaved himself in form, Mr. Langridge would set him lines in blissful ignorance of the fact that he would not be there next day to show them up. At the beginning of the following term, moreover, he would not be in Mr. Langridge's form, for he was certain of his move up.

He acted accordingly.

He spent the earlier part of Wednesday morning in breaches of the peace. Mr. Langridge, instead of pulling him up, put him on to translate; Dunstable went on to translate. As he had not prepared the lesson and was not an adept at construing unseen, his performance was poor.

After a minute and a half, the form-master wearied.

"Have you looked at this, Dunstable?" he asked.

There was a time-honoured answer to this question.

"Yes, sir," he said.

Public-school ethics do not demand that you should reply truthfully to the spirit of a question. The letter of it is all that requires attention. Dunstable had *looked* at the lesson. He was looking at it then. Masters should practise exactness of speech. A certain form at Harrow were in the habit of walking across a copy of a Latin author before morning-school. They could then say with truth that they "had been over it." This is not an isolated case.

"Go on," said Mr. Langridge.

Dunstable smiled as he did so.

Mr. Langridge was annoyed.

"What are you laughing at? What do you mean by it? Stand up. You will write out the lesson in Latin and English, and show it up to me by four this afternoon. I know what you are thinking. You imagine that because this is the end of the term you can do as you please, but you will find yourself mistaken. Mind—by four o'clock."

At four o'clock Dunstable was enjoying an excellent tea in Green Street, Park Lane, and telling his mother that he had had a most enjoyable term, marred by no unpleasantness whatever. His holidays were sweetened by the thought of Mr. Langridge's baffled wrath on discovering the true inwardness of the recent episode.

When he returned to Locksley at the beginning of the winter term, he was at once made aware that that episode was not to be considered closed. On the first evening, Mr. Day, his housemaster, sent for him.

"Well, Dunstable," he said, "where is that imposition?"

Dunstable affected ignorance.

"Please, sir, you set me no imposition."

"No, Dunstable, no." Mr. Day peered at him gravely through his spectacles. "*I* set you no imposition; but Mr. Langridge did."

Dunstable imitated that eminent tactician, Br'er Rabbit. He "lay low and said nuffin."

"Surely," continued Mr. Day, in tones of mild reproach, "you did not think that you could take Mr. Langridge in?"

Dunstable rather thought he *had* taken Mr. Langridge in; but he made no reply.

"Well," said Mr. Day. "I must set you some punishment. I shall give the butler instructions to hand you a note from me at three o'clock to-morrow." (The next day was a half-holiday.) "In that note you will find indicated what I wish you to write out."

Why this comic-opera secret-society business, Dunstable wondered. Then it dawned upon him. Mr. Day wished to break up his half-holiday thoroughly.

That afternoon Dunstable retired in disgust to his study to brood over his wrongs; to him entered Charles, his friend, one C. J. Linton, to wit, of Seymour's, a very hearty sportsman.

"Good," said Linton. "Didn't think I should find you in. Thought you might have gone off somewhere as it's such a ripping day. Tell you what we'll do. Scull a mile or two up the river and have tea somewhere."

"I should like to awfully," said Dunstable, "but I'm afraid I can't."

And he explained Mr. Day's ingenious scheme for preventing him from straying that afternoon.

"Rot, isn't it," he said.

"Beastly. Wouldn't have thought old Day had it in him. But I'll tell you what," he said. "Do the impot now, and then you'll be able to start at three sharp, and we shall get in a good time on the river. Day always sets the same thing. I've known scores of chaps get impots from him, and they all had to do the Greek numerals. He's mad on the Greek numerals. Never does anything else. You'll be as safe as anything if you do them. Buck up, I'll help."

They accordingly sat down there and then. By three o'clock an imposing array of sheets of foolscap covered with badly-written Greek lay on the study table.

"That ought to be enough," said Linton, laying down his pen. "He can't set you more than we've done, I should think."

"Rummy how alike our writing looks," said Dunstable, collecting the sheets and examining them. "You can hardly tell which is which even when you know. Well, there goes three. My watch is slow, as it always is. I'll go and get that note."

Two minutes later he returned, full of abusive references to Mr. Day. The crafty pedagogue appeared to have foreseen Dunstable's attempt to circumvent him by doing the Greek numerals on the chance of his setting them. The imposition he had set in his note was ten pages of irregular verbs, and they were to be shown up in his study before five o'clock. Linton's programme for the afternoon was out of the question now. But he loyally gave up any other plans which he might have formed in order to help Dunstable with his irregular verbs. Dunstable was too disgusted with fate to be properly grateful.

"And the worst of it is," he said, as they adjourned for tea at half-past four, having deposited the verbs on Mr. Day's table, "that all those numerals will be wasted now."

"I should keep them, though," said Linton. "They may come in useful. You never know."

Towards the end of the second week of term Fate, by way of compensation, allowed Dunstable a distinct stroke of luck. Mr. Forman, the master of his new form, set him a hundred lines of Virgil, and told him to show them up next day. To Dunstable's delight, the next day passed without mention of them; and when the day after that went by, and still nothing was said, he came to the conclusion that Mr. Forman had forgotten all about them.

Which was indeed the case. Mr. Forman was engaged in editing a new edition of the "Bacchae," and was apt to be absent-minded in consequence. So Dunstable, with a glad smile, hove the lines into a cupboard in his study to keep company with the Greek numerals which he had done for Mr. Day, and went out to play fives with Linton.

Linton, curiously enough, had also had a stroke of luck in a rather similar way. He told Dunstable about it as they strolled back to the houses after their game.

"Bit of luck this afternoon," he said. "You remember Appleby setting me a hundred-and-fifty the day before yesterday? Well, I showed them up to-day, and he looked through them and chucked them into the waste-paper basket under his desk. I thought at the time I hadn't seen him muck them up at all with his pencil, which is his usual game, so after he had gone at the end of school I nipped to the basket and fished them out. They were as good as new, so I saved them up in case I get any more."

Dunstable hastened to tell of his own good fortune. Linton was impressed by the coincidence.

"I tell you what," he said, "we score either way. Because if we never get any more lines——"

Dunstable laughed.

"Yes, I know," Linton went on, "we're bound to. But even supposing we don't, what we've got in stock needn't be wasted."

"I don't see that," said Dunstable. "Going to have 'em bound in cloth and published? Or were you thinking of framing them?"

"Why, don't you see? Sell them, of course. There are dozens of chaps in the school who would be glad of a few hundred lines cheap."

"It wouldn't work. They'd be spotted."

"Rot. It's been done before, and nobody said anything. A chap in Seymour's who left last Easter sold all his stock lines by auction on the last day of term.

They were Virgil mostly and Greek numerals. They sold like hot cakes. There were about five hundred of them altogether. And I happen to know that every word of them has been given up and passed all right."

"Well, I shall keep mine," said Dunstable. "I am sure to want all the lines in stock that I can get. I used to think Langridge was fairly bad in the way of impots, but Forman takes the biscuit easily. It seems to be a sort of hobby of his. You can't stop him."

But it was not until the middle of preparation that the great idea flashed upon Dunstable's mind.

It was the simplicity of the thing that took his breath away. That and its possibilities. This was the idea. Why not start a Lines Trust in the school? An agency for supplying lines at moderate rates to all who desired them? There did not seem to be a single flaw in the scheme. He and Linton between them could turn out enough material in a week to give the Trust a good working capital. And as for the risk of detection when customers came to show up the goods supplied to them, that was very slight. As has been pointed out before, there was practically one handwriting common to the whole school when it came to writing lines. It resembled the movements of a fly that had fallen into an ink-pot, and subsequently taken a little brisk exercise on a sheet of foolscap by way of restoring the circulation. Then, again, the attitude of the master to whom the lines were shown was not likely to be critical.

So that everything seemed in favour of Dunstable's scheme.

Linton, to whom he confided it, was inclined to scoff at first, but when he had had the beauties of the idea explained to him at length, became an enthusiastic supporter of the scheme.

"But," he objected, "it'll take up all our time. Is it worth it? We can't spend every afternoon sweating away at impots for other people."

"It's all right," said Dunstable, "I've thought of that. We shall need to pitch in pretty hard for about a week or ten days. That will give us a good big stock, and after that if we turn out a hundred each every day it will be all right. A hundred's not much fag if you spread them over a day."

Linton admitted that this was sound, and the Locksley Lines Supplying Trust, Ltd., set to work in earnest.

It must not be supposed that the Agency left a great deal to chance. The writing of lines in advance may seem a very speculative business; but both Dunstable and Linton had had a wide experience of Locksley masters, and the methods of the same when roused, and they were thus enabled to reduce the element of chance to a minimum. They knew, for example, that Mr. Day's favourite imposition was the Greek numerals, and that in nine cases out of ten that would be what the youth who had dealings with him would need to ask for from the Lines Trust. Mr.

Appleby, on the other hand, invariably set Virgil. The oldest inhabitant had never known him to depart from this custom. For the French masters extracts from the works of Victor Hugo would probably pass muster.

A week from the date of the above conversation, everyone in the school, with the exception of the prefects and the sixth form, found in his desk on arriving at his form-room a printed slip of paper. (Spiking, the stationer in the High Street, had printed it.) It was nothing less than the prospectus of the new Trust. It set forth in glowing terms the advantages offered by the agency. Dunstable had written it—he had a certain amount of skill with his pen—and Linton had suggested subtle and captivating additions. The whole presented rather a striking appearance.

The document was headed with the name of the Trust in large letters. Under this came a number of "scare headlines" such as:

SEE WHAT YOU SAVE!

NO MORE WORRY!

PEACE, PERFECT PEACE!

*WHY DO LINES WHEN WE DO THEM
FOR YOU?*

Then came the real prospectus:

The Locksley Lines Supplying Trust, Ltd. has been instituted to meet the growing demand for lines and other impositions. While there are masters at our public schools there will always be lines.

At Locksley the crop of masters has always flourished—and still flourishes—very rankly, and the demand for lines has greatly taxed the powers of those to whom has been assigned the task of supplying them.

It is for the purpose of affording relief to these that the Lines Trust has been formed. It is proposed that all orders for lines shall be supplied out of our vast stock. Our charges are moderate, and vary between threepence and sixpence per hundred lines. The higher charge is made for Greek impositions, which, for obvious reasons, entail a greater degree of labour on our large and efficient staff of writers.

All orders, which will be promptly executed, should be forwarded to Mr. P. A. Dunstable, 6 College Grounds, Locksley, or to Mr. C. J. Linton, 10 College Grounds, Locksley. Payment must be inclosed with order, or the latter will not be executed. Under no conditions will notes of hand or cheques be accepted as legal tender. There is no trust about us except the name.

Come in your thousands. We have lines for all. If the Trust's stock of lines were to be placed end to end it would reach part of the way to London. "You pay the threepence. We do the rest."

Then a blank space, after which came a few "unsolicited testimonials":

"Lower Fifth" writes: "I was set two hundred lines of Virgil on Saturday last at one o'clock. Having laid in a supply from your agency I was enabled to show them up at five minutes past one.

The master who gave me the commission was unable to restrain his admiration at the rapidity and neatness of my work. You may make what use of this you please."

"Dexter's House" writes: "Please send me one hundred (100) lines from Aeneid, Book Two. Mr. Dexter was so delighted with the last I showed him that he has asked me to do some more."

"Enthusiast" writes: "Thank you for your Greek numerals. Day took them without blinking. So beautifully were they executed that I can hardly believe even now that I did not write them myself."

There could be no doubt about the popularity of the Trust. It caught on instantly.

Nothing else was discussed in the form-rooms at the quarter to eleven interval, and in the houses after lunch it was the sole topic of conversation. Dunstable and Linton were bombarded with questions and witticisms of the near personal sort. To the latter they replied with directness, to the former evasively.

"What's it all *about?*" someone would ask, fluttering the leaflet before Dunstable's unmoved face.

"You should read it carefully," Dunstable would reply. "It's all there."

"But what are you playing at?"

"We tried to make it clear to the meanest intelligence. Sorry you can't understand it."

While at the same time Linton, in his form-room, would be explaining to excited inquirers that he was sorry, but it was impossible to reply to their query as to who was running the Trust. He was not at liberty to reveal business secrets. Suffice it that there the lines were, waiting to be bought, and he was there to sell them. So that if anybody cared to lay in a stock, large or small, according to taste, would he kindly walk up and deposit the necessary coin?

But here the public showed an unaccountable disinclination to deal. It was gratifying to have acquaintances coming up and saying admiringly: "You are an ass, you know," as if they were paying the highest of compliments—as, indeed, they probably imagined that they were. All this was magnificent, but it was not business. Dunstable and Linton felt that the whole attitude of the public towards the new enterprise was wrong. Locksley seemed to regard the Trust as a huge joke, and its prospectus as a literary *jeu d'esprit*.

In fact, it looked very much as if—from a purely commercial point of view—the great Lines Supplying Trust was going to be what is known in theatrical circles as a frost.

For two whole days the public refused to bite, and Dunstable and Linton, turning over the stacks of lines in their studies, thought gloomily that this world is no place for original enterprise.

Then things began to move.

It was quite an accident that started them. Jackson, of Dexter's, was teaing with Linton, and, as was his habit, was giving him a condensed history of his life since he last saw him. In the course of this he touched on a small encounter with M. Gaudinois which had occurred that afternoon.

"So I got two pages of 'Quatre-Vingt Treize' to write," he concluded, "for doing practically nothing."

All Jackson's impositions, according to him, were given him for doing practically nothing. Now and then he got them for doing literally nothing—when he ought to have been doing form-work.

"Done 'em?" asked Linton.

"Not yet; no," replied Jackson. "More tea, please."

"What you want to do, then," said Linton, "is to apply to the Locksley Lines Supplying Trust. That's what you must do."

"You needn't rot a chap on a painful subject," protested Jackson.

"I wasn't rotting," said Linton. "Why don't you apply to the Lines Trust?"

"Then do you mean to say that there really is such a thing?" Jackson said incredulously. "Why I thought it was all a rag."

"I know you did. It's the rotten sort of thing you would think. Rag, by Jove! Look at this. Now do you understand that this is a genuine concern?"

He got up and went to the cupboard which filled the space between the stove and the bookshelf. From this resting-place he extracted a great pile of manuscript and dumped it down on the table with a bang which caused a good deal of Jackson's tea to spring from its native cup on to its owner's trousers.

"When you've finished," protested Jackson, mopping himself with a handkerchief that had seen better days.

"Sorry. But look at these. What did you say your impot was? Oh, I remember. Here you are. Two pages of 'Quatre-Vingt Treize.' I don't know which two pages, but I suppose any will do."

Jackson was amazed.

"Great Scott! what a wad of stuff! When did you do it all?"

"Oh, at odd times. Dunstable's got just as much over at Day's. So you see the Trust is a jolly big show. Here are your two pages. That looks just like your scrawl, doesn't it? These would be fourpence in the ordinary way, but you can have 'em for nothing this time."

"Oh, I say," said Jackson gratefully, "that's awfully good of you."

After that the Locksley Lines Supplying Trust, Ltd. went ahead with a rush. The brilliant success which attended its first specimen—M. Gaudinois took Jackson's imposition without a murmur—promoted confidence in the public, and they rushed to buy. Orders poured in from all the houses, and by the middle of the term the organisers of the scheme were able to divide a substantial sum.

"How are you getting on round your way?" asked Linton of Dunstable at the end of the sixth week of term.

"Ripping. Selling like hot cakes."

"So are mine," said Linton. "I've almost come to the end of my stock. I ought to have written some more, but I've been a bit slack lately."

"Yes, buck up. We must keep a lot in hand."

"I say, did you hear that about Merrett in our house?" asked Linton.

"What about him?"

"Why, he tried to start a rival show. Wrote a prospectus and everything. But it didn't catch on a bit. The only chap who bought any of his lines was young Shoeblossom. He wanted a couple of hundred for Appleby. Appleby was on to them like bricks. Spotted Shoeblossom hadn't written them, and asked who had. He wouldn't say, so he got them doubled. Everyone in the house is jolly sick with Merrett. They think he ought to have owned up."

"Did that smash up Merrett's show? Is he going to turn out any more?"

"Rather not. Who'd buy 'em?"

It would have been better for the Lines Supplying Trust if Merrett had not received this crushing blow and had been allowed to carry on a rival business on legitimate lines. Locksley was conservative in its habits, and would probably have continued to support the old firm.

As it was, the baffled Merrett, a youth of vindictive nature, brooded over his defeat, and presently hit upon a scheme whereby things might be levelled up.

One afternoon, shortly before lock-up, Dunstable was surprised by the advent of Linton to his study in a bruised and dishevelled condition. One of his expressive eyes was closed and blackened. He also wore what is known in ring circles as a thick ear.

"What on earth's up?" inquired Dunstable, amazed at these phenomena. "Have you been scrapping?"

"Yes—Merrett—I won. What are you up to— writing lines? You may as well save yourself the trouble. They won't be any good." Dunstable stared.

"The Trust's bust," said Linton.

He never wasted words in moments of emotion.

"What!"

"'Bust' was what I said. That beast Merrett gave the show away."

"What did he do? Surely he didn't tell a master?"

"Well, he did the next thing to it. He hauled out that prospectus, and started reading it in form. I watched him do it. He kept it under the desk and made a foul row, laughing over it. Appleby couldn't help spotting him. Of course, he told him to bring him what he was reading. Up went Merrett with the prospectus."

"Was Appleby sick?"

"I don't believe he was, really. At least, he laughed when he read the thing. But he hauled me up after school and gave me a long jaw, and made me take all the lines I'd got to his house. He burnt them. I had it out with Merrett just now. He swears he didn't mean to get the thing spotted, but I knew he did."

"Where did you scrag him!"

"In the dormitory. He chucked it after the third round."

There was a knock at the door.

"Come in," shouted Dunstable.

Buxton appeared, a member of Appleby's house.

"Oh, Dunstable, Appleby wants to see you."

"All right," said Dunstable wearily.

Mr. Appleby was in facetious mood. He chaffed Dunstable genially about his prospectus, and admitted that it had amused him. Dunstable smiled without enjoyment. It was a good thing, perhaps, that Mr. Appleby saw the humorous rather than the lawless side of the Trust; but all the quips in the world could not save that institution from ruin.

Presently Mr. Appleby's manner changed. "I am a funny dog, I know," he seemed to say; "but duty is duty, and must be done."

"How many lines have you at your house, Dunstable?" he asked.

"About eight hundred, sir."

"Then you had better write me eight hundred lines, and show them up to me in this room at—shall we say at ten minutes to five? It is now a quarter to, so that you will have plenty of time."

Dunstable went, and returned five minutes later, bearing an armful of manuscript.

"I don't think I shall need to count them," said Mr. Appleby. "Kindly take them in batches of ten sheets, and tear them in half, Dunstable."

"Yes, sir."

The last sheet fluttered in two sections into the surfeited waste-paper basket.

"It's an awful waste, sir," said Dunstable regretfully.

Mr. Appleby beamed.

"We must, however," he said, "always endeavour to look on the bright side, Dunstable. The writing of these eight hundred lines will have given you a fine grip of the rhythm of Virgil, the splendid prose of Victor Hugo, and the unstudied majesty of the Greek Numerals. Good-night, Dunstable."

"Good-night, sir," said the President of the Locksley Lines Supplying Trust, Ltd.

The Autograph Hunters

Dunstable had his reasons for wishing to obtain Mr. Montagu Watson's autograph, but admiration for that gentleman's novels was not one of them.

It was nothing to him that critics considered Mr. Watson one of the most remarkable figures in English literature since Scott. If you had told him of this, he would merely have wondered in his coarse, material way how much Mr. Watson gave the critics for saying so. To the reviewer of the *Weekly Booklover* the great man's latest effort, "The Soul of Anthony Carrington" (Popgood and Grooly: 6s.) seemed "a work that speaks eloquently in every line of a genius that time cannot wither nor custom stale." To Dunstable, who got it out of the school library, where it had been placed at the request of a literary prefect, and read the first eleven pages, it seemed rot, and he said as much to the librarian on returning it.

Yet he was very anxious to get the novelist's autograph. The fact was that Mr. Day, his house-master, a man whose private life was in other ways unstained by vicious habits, collected autographs. Also Mr. Day had behaved in a square manner towards

Dunstable on several occasions in the past, and Dunstable, always ready to punish bad behaviour in a master, was equally anxious to reward and foster any good trait which he might exhibit.

On the occasion of the announcement that Mr. Watson had taken the big white house near Chesterton, a couple of miles from the school, Mr. Day had expressed in Dunstable's hearing a wish that he could add that celebrity's signature to his collection. Dunstable had instantly determined to play the part of a benevolent Providence. He would get the autograph and present it to the house-master, as who should say, "see what comes of being good." It would be pleasant to observe the innocent joy of the recipient, his child-like triumph, and his amazement at the donor's ingenuity in securing the treasure. A touching scene—well worth the trouble involved in the quest.

And there would be trouble. For Mr. Montagu Watson was notoriously a foe to the autograph-hunter. His curt, type-written replies (signed by a secretary) had damped the ardour of scores of brave men and—more or less—fair women. A genuine Montagu Watson was a prize in the autograph market.

Dunstable was a man of action. When Mark, the boot-boy at Day's, carried his burden of letters to the post that evening, there nestled among them one addressed to M. Watson, Esq., The White House, Chesterton. Looking at it casually, few of his friends would have recognised Dunstable's handwriting. For it had seemed good to that man of guile to adopt for the occasion the role of a backward youth of twelve years old. He thought tender years might touch Mr. Watson's heart.

This was the letter:

Dear Sir,—I am only a littel boy, but I think your

books ripping. I often wonder how you think of it all. Will you please send me your ortograf? I like your books very much. I have named my white rabit Montagu after you. I punched Jones II in the eye to-day becos he didn't like your books. I have spent the only penny I have on the stampe for this letter which I might have spent on tuck. I want to be like Maltby in "The Soul of Anthony Carrington" when I grow up.

Your sincere reader,

P. A. Dunstable.

It was a little unfortunate, perhaps, that he selected Maltby as his ideal character. That gentleman was considered by critics a masterly portrait of the cynical *roui*. But it was the only name he remembered.

"Hot stuff!" said Dunstable to himself, as he closed the envelope.

"Little beast!" said Mr. Watson to himself as he opened it. It arrived by the morning post, and he never felt really himself till after breakfast.

"Here, Morrison," he said to his secretary, later in the morning: "just answer this, will you? The usual thing—thanks and most deeply grateful, y'know."

Next day the following was included in Dunstable's correspondence:

Mr. Montagu Watson presents his compliments to Mr. P. A. Dunstable, and begs to thank him for all the kind things he says about his work in his letter of the 18th inst., for which he is deeply grateful.

"Foiled!" said Dunstable, and went off to Seymour's to see his friend Linton.

"Got any notepaper?" he asked.

"Heaps," said Linton. "Why? Want some?"

"Then get out a piece. I want to dictate a letter."

Linton stared.

"What's up? Hurt your hand?"

Dunstable explained.

"Day collects autographs, you know, and he wants Montagu Watson's badly. Pining away, and all that sort of thing. Won't smile until he gets it. I had a shot at it yesterday, and got this."

Linton inspected the document.

"So I can't send up another myself, you see."

"Why worry?"

"Oh, I'd like to put Day one up. He's not been bad this term. Come on."

"All right. Let her rip."

Dunstable let her rip.

Dear Sir,—I cannot refrain from writing to tell you what an inestimable comfort your novels have been to me during years of sore tribulation and distress——

"Look here," interrupted Linton with decision at this point. "If you think I'm going to shove my name at the end of this rot, you're making the mistake of a lifetime."

"Of course not. You're a widow who has lost two sons in South Africa. We'll think of a good name afterwards. Ready?

"Ever since my darling Charles Herbert and Percy Lionel were taken from me in that dreadful war, I have turned for consolation to the pages of 'The Soul of Anthony Carrington' and——"

"What, another?" asked Linton.

"There's one called 'Pancakes.'"

"Sure? Sounds rummy."

"That's all right. You have to get a queer title nowadays if you want to sell a book."

"Go on, then. Jam it down."

"——and 'Pancakes.' I hate to bother you, but if you could send me your autograph I should be more grateful than words can say.

Yours admiringly."

"What's a good name? How would Dorothy Maynard do?"

"You want something more aristocratic. What price Hilda Foulke-Ponsonby?"

Dunstable made no objection, and Linton signed the letter with a flourish.

They installed Mrs. Foulke-Ponsonby at Spiking's in the High Street. It was not a very likely address for a lady whose blood was presumably of the bluest, but they could think of none except that obliging stationer who would take in letters for them.

There was a letter for Mrs. Foulke-Ponsonby next day. Whatever his other defects as a correspondent, Mr. Watson was at least prompt with his responses.

Mr. Montagu Watson presented his compliments, and was deeply grateful for all the kind things Mrs. Foulke-Ponsonby had said about his work in her letter of the 19th inst. He was, however, afraid that he scarcely deserved them. Her opportunities of deriving consolation from "The Soul of Anthony Carrington" had been limited by the fact that that book had only been published ten days before: while, as for "Pancakes," to which she had referred in such flattering terms, he feared that another author must have the credit of any refreshment her bereaved spirit might have extracted from that volume, for he had written no work of such a name. His own "Pan Wakes" would, he hoped, administer an equal quantity of balm.

Mr. Secretary Morrison had slept badly on the night before he wrote this letter, and had expended some venom upon its composition.

"Sold again!" said Dunstable.

"You'd better chuck it now. It's no good," said Linton.

"I'll have another shot. Then I'll try and think of something else."

Two days later Mr. Morrison replied to Mr. Edgar Habbesham-Morley, of 3a, Green Street, Park Lane, to the effect that Mr. Montagu Watson was deeply grateful for all the kind things, etc.——

3a, Green Street was Dunstable's home address.

At this juncture the Watson-Dunstable correspondence ceases, and the relations become more personal.

On the afternoon of the twenty-third of the month, Mr. Watson, taking a meditative stroll through the wood which formed part of his property, was infuriated by the sight of a boy.

He was not a man who was fond of boys even in their proper place, and the sight of one in the middle of his wood, prancing lightly about among the nesting pheasants, stirred his never too placid mind to its depths.

He shouted.

The apparition paused.

"Here! Hi! you boy!"

"Sir?" said the stripling, with a winning smile, lifting his cap with the air of a D'Orsay.

"What business have you in my wood?"

"Not business," corrected the visitor, "pleasure."

"Come here!" shrilled the novelist.

The stranger receded coyly.

Mr. Watson advanced at the double.

His quarry dodged behind a tree.

For five minutes the great man devoted his powerful mind solely to the task of catching his visitor.

The latter, however, proved as elusive as the point of a half-formed epigram, and at the end of the five minutes he was no longer within sight.

Mr. Watson went off and addressed his keeper in terms which made that worthy envious for a week.

"It's eddication," he said subsequently to a friend at the "Cowslip Inn." "You and me couldn't talk like that. It wants eddication."

For the next few days the keeper's existence was enlivened by visits from what appeared to be a most enthusiastic bird's-nester. By no other theory could he account for it. Only a boy with a collection to support would run such risks.

To the keeper's mind the human boy up to the age of twenty or so had no object in life except to collect eggs. After twenty, of course, he took to poaching. This was a boy of about seventeen.

On the fifth day he caught him, and conducted him into the presence of Mr. Montagu Watson.

Mr. Watson was brief and to the point. He recognised his visitor as the boy for whose benefit he had made himself stiff for two days.

The keeper added further damaging facts.

"Bin here every day, he 'as, sir, for the last week. Well, I says to myself, supposition is he'll come once too often. He'll come once too often, I says. And then, I says, I'll cotch him. And I cotched him."

The keeper's narrative style had something of the classic simplicity of Julius Caesar's.

Mr. Watson bit his pen.

"What you boys come for I can't understand," he said irritably. "You're from the school, of course?"

"Yes," said the captive.

"Well, I shall report you to your house-master. What is your name?"

"Dunstable."

"Your house?"

"Day's."

"Very good. That is all."

Dunstable retired.

His next appearance in public life was in Mr. Day's study. Mr. Day had sent for him after preparation. He held a letter in his hand, and he looked annoyed.

"Come in, Dunstable. I have just received a letter complaining of you. It seems that you have been trespassing."

"Yes, sir."

"I am surprised, Dunstable, that a sensible boy like you should have done such a foolish thing. It seems so objectless. You know how greatly the head-master dislikes any sort of friction between the school and the neighbours, and yet you deliberately trespass in Mr. Watson's wood."

"I'm very sorry, sir."

"I have had a most indignant letter from him—you may see what he says. You do not deny it?"

Dunstable ran his eye over the straggling, untidy sentences.

"No, sir. It's quite true."

"In that case I shall have to punish you severely. You will write me out the Greek numerals ten times, and show them up to me on Tuesday."

"Yes, sir."

"That will do."

At the door Dunstable paused.

"Well, Dunstable?" said Mr. Day.

"Er—I'm glad you've got his autograph after all, sir," he said.

Then he closed the door.

As he was going to bed that night, Dunstable met the house-master on the stairs.

"Dunstable," said Mr. Day.

"Yes, sir."

"On second thoughts, it would be better if, instead of the Greek numerals ten times, you wrote me the first ode of the first book of Horace. The numerals would be a little long, perhaps."

Pillingshot, Detective

Life at St. Austin's was rendered somewhat hollow and burdensome for Pillingshot by the fact that he fagged for Scott. Not that Scott was the Beetle-Browed Bully in any way. Far from it. He showed a kindly interest in Pillingshot's welfare, and sometimes even did his Latin verses for him. But the noblest natures have flaws, and Scott's was no exception. He was by way of being a humorist, and Pillingshot, with his rather serious outlook on life, was puzzled and inconvenienced by this.

It was through this defect in Scott's character that Pillingshot first became a detective.

He was toasting muffins at the study fire one evening, while Scott, seated on two chairs and five cushions, read "Sherlock Holmes," when the Prefect laid down his book and fixed him with an earnest eye.

"Do you know, Pillingshot," he said, "you've got a bright, intelligent face. I shouldn't wonder if you weren't rather clever. Why do you hide your light under a bushel?"

Pillingshot grunted.

"We must find some way of advertising you. Why don't you go in for a Junior Scholarship?"

"Too old," said Pillingshot with satisfaction.

"Senior, then?"

"Too young."

"I believe by sitting up all night and swotting——"

"Here, I say!" said Pillingshot, alarmed.

"You've got no enterprise," said Scott sadly. "What are those? Muffins? Well, well, I suppose I had better try and peck a bit."

He ate four in rapid succession, and resumed his scrutiny of Pillingshot's countenance.

"The great thing," he said, "is to find out your special line. Till then we are working in the dark. Perhaps it's music? Singing? Sing me a bar or two."

Pillingshot wriggled uncomfortably.

"Left your music at home?" said Scott. "Never mind, then. Perhaps it's all for the best. What are those? Still muffins? Hand me another. After all, one must keep one's strength up. You can have one if you like."

Pillingshot's face brightened. He became more affable. He chatted.

"There's rather a row on downstairs," he said. "In the junior day-room."

"There always is," said Scott. "If it grows too loud, I shall get in amongst them with a swagger-stick. I attribute half my success at bringing off late-cuts to the practice I have had in the junior day-room. It keeps the wrist supple."

"I don't mean that sort of row. It's about Evans."

"What about Evans?"

"He's lost a sovereign."

"Silly young ass."

Pillingshot furtively helped himself to another muffin.

"He thinks some one's taken it," he said.

"What! Stolen it?"

Pillingshot nodded.

"What makes him think that?"

"He doesn't see how else it could have gone."

"Oh, I don't—By Jove!"

Scott sat up with some excitement.

"I've got it," he said. "I knew we should hit on it sooner or later. Here's a field for your genius. You shall be a detective. Pillingshot, I hand this case over to you. I employ you."

Pillingshot gaped.

"I feel certain that's your line. I've often noticed you walking over to school, looking exactly like a blood-hound. Get to work. As a start you'd better fetch Evans up here and question him."

"But, look here———"

"Buck up, man, buck up. Don't you know that every moment is precious?"

Evans, a small, stout youth, was not disposed to be reticent. The gist of his rambling statement was as follows. Rich uncle. Impecunious nephew. Visit of former to latter. Handsome tip, one sovereign. Impecunious nephew pouches sovereign, and it vanishes.

"And I call it beastly rot," concluded Evans volubly. "And if I could find the cad who's pinched it, I'd jolly well———"

"Less of it," said Scott. "Now, then, Pillingshot, I'll begin this thing, just to start you off. What makes you think the quid has been stolen, Evans?"

"Because I jolly well know it has."

"What you jolly well know isn't evidence. We must thresh this thing out. To begin with, where did you last see it?"

"When I put it in my pocket."

"Good. Make a note of that, Pillingshot. Where's your notebook? Not got one? Here you are then. You can tear out the first few pages, the ones I've written on. Ready? Carry on, Evans. When?"

"When what?"

"When did you put it in your pocket?"

"Yesterday afternoon."

"What time?"

"About five."

"Same pair of bags you're wearing now?"

"No, my cricket bags. I was playing at the nets when my uncle came."

"Ah! Cricket bags? Put it down, Pillingshot. That's a clue. Work on it. Where are they?"

"They've gone to the wash."

"About time, too. I noticed them. How do you know the quid didn't go to the wash as well?"

"I turned both the pockets inside out."

"Any hole in the pocket?"

"No."

"Well, when did you take off the bags? Did you sleep in them?"

"I wore 'em till bed-time, and then shoved them on a chair by the side of the bed. It wasn't till next morning that I remembered the quid was in them——"

"But it wasn't," objected Scott.

"I thought it was. It ought to have been."

"He thought it was. That's a clue, young Pillingshot. Work on it. Well?"

"Well, when I went to take the quid out of my cricket bags, it wasn't there."

"What time was that?"

"Half-past seven this morning."

"What time did you go to bed?"

"Ten."

"Then the theft occurred between the hours of ten and seven-thirty. Mind you, I'm giving you a jolly good leg-up, young Pillingshot. But as it's your first case I don't mind. That'll be all from you, Evans. Pop off."

Evans disappeared. Scott turned to the detective.

"Well, young Pillingshot," he said, "what do you make of it?"

"I don't know."

"What steps do you propose to take?"

"I don't know."

"You're a lot of use, aren't you? As a start, you'd better examine the scene of the robbery, I should say."

Pillingshot reluctantly left the room.

"Well?" said Scott, when he returned. "Any clues?"

"No."

"You thoroughly examined the scene of the robbery?"

"I looked under the bed."

"*Under* the bed? What's the good of that? Did you go over every inch of the strip of carpet leading to the chair with a magnifying-glass?"

"Hadn't got a magnifying-glass."

"Then you'd better buck up and get one, if you're going to be a detective. Do you think Sherlock Holmes ever moved a step without his? Not much. Well, anyhow. Did you find any foot-prints or tobacco-ash?"

"There was a jolly lot of dust about."

"Did you preserve a sample?"

"No."

"My word, you've a lot to learn. Now, weighing the evidence, does anything strike you?"

"No."

"You're a bright sort of sleuth-hound, aren't you! It seems to me I'm doing all the work on this case. I'll have to give you another leg-up. Considering the time when the quid disappeared, I should say that somebody in the dormitory must have collared it. How many fellows are there in Evans' dormitory?"

"I don't know."

"Cut along and find out."

The detective reluctantly trudged off once more.

"Well?" said Scott, on his return.

"Seven," said Pillingshot. "Counting Evans."

"We needn't count Evans. If he's ass enough to steal his own quids, he deserves to lose them. Who are the other six?"

"There's Trent. He's prefect."

"The Napoleon of Crime. Watch his every move. Yes?"

"Simms."

"A dangerous man. Sinister to the core."

"And Green, Berkeley, Hanson, and Daubeny."

"Every one of them well known to the police. Why, the place is a perfect Thieves' Kitchen. Look here, we must act swiftly, young Pillingshot. This is a black business. We'll take them in alphabetical order. Run and fetch Berkeley."

Berkeley, interrupted in a game of Halma, came unwillingly.

"Now then, Pillingshot, put your questions," said Scott. "This is a black business, Berkeley. Young Evans has lost a sovereign——"

"If you think I've taken his beastly quid——!" said Berkeley warmly.

"Make a note that, on being questioned, the man Berkeley exhibited suspicious emotion. Go on. Jam it down."

Pillingshot reluctantly entered the statement under Berkeley's indignant gaze.

"Now then, carry on."

"You know, it's all rot," protested Pillingshot. "I never said Berkeley had anything to do with it."

"Never mind. Ask him what his movements were on the night of the—what was yesterday?—on the night of the sixteenth of July."

Pillingshot put the question nervously.

"I was in bed, of course, you silly ass."

"Were you asleep?" inquired Scott.

"Of course I was."

"Then how do you know what you were doing? Pillingshot, make a note of the fact that the man Berkeley's statement was confused and contradictory. It's a clue. Work on it. Who's next? Daubeny. Berkeley, send Daubeny up here."

"All right, Pillingshot, you wait," was Berkeley's exit speech.

Daubeny, when examined, exhibited the same suspicious emotion that Berkeley had shown; and Hanson, Simms, and Green behaved in a precisely similar manner.

"This," said Scott, "somewhat complicates the case. We must have further clues. You'd better pop off now, Pillingshot. I've got a Latin Prose to do. Bring me reports of your progress daily, and don't overlook the importance of trifles. Why, in 'Silver Blaze' it was a burnt match that first put Holmes on the scent."

Entering the junior day-room with some apprehension, the sleuth-hound found an excited gathering of suspects waiting to interview him.

One sentiment animated the meeting. Each of the five wanted to know what Pillingshot meant by it.

"What's the row?" queried interested spectators, rallying round.

"That cad Pillingshot's been accusing us of bagging Evans' quid."

"What's Scott got to do with it?" inquired one of the spectators.

Pillingshot explained his position.

"All the same," said Daubeny, "you needn't have dragged us into it."

"I couldn't help it. He made me."

"Awful ass, Scott," admitted Green.

Pillingshot welcomed this sign that the focus of popular indignation was being shifted.

"Shoving himself into other people's business," grumbled Pillingshot.

"Trying to be funny," Berkeley summed up.

"Rotten at cricket, too."

"Can't play a yorker for nuts."

"See him drop that sitter on Saturday?"

So that was all right. As far as the junior day-room was concerned, Pillingshot felt himself vindicated.

But his employer was less easily satisfied. Pillingshot had hoped that by the next day he would have forgotten the subject. But, when he went into the study to get tea ready, up it came again.

"Any clues yet, Pillingshot?"

Pillingshot had to admit that there were none.

"Hullo, this won't do. You must bustle about. You must get your nose to the trail. Have you cross-examined Trent yet? No? Well, there you are, then. Nip off and do it now."

"But, I say, Scott! He's a prefect!"

"In the dictionary of crime," said Scott sententiously, "there is no such word as prefect. All are alike. Go and take down Trent's statement."

To tax a prefect with having stolen a sovereign was a task at which Pillingshot's imagination boggled. He went to Trent's study in a sort of dream.

A hoarse roar answered his feeble tap. There was no doubt about Trent being in. Inspection revealed the fact that the prefect was working and evidently ill-attuned to conversation. He wore a haggard look and his eye, as it caught that of the collector of statements, was dangerous.

"Well?" said Trent, scowling murderously.

Pillingshot's legs felt perfectly boneless.

"*Well?*" said Trent.

Pillingshot yammered.

"*Well?*"

The roar shook the window, and Pillingshot's presence of mind deserted him altogether.

"Have you bagged a sovereign?" he asked.

There was an awful silence, during which the detective, his limbs suddenly becoming active again, banged the door, and shot off down the passage.

He re-entered Scott's study at the double.

"Well?" said Scott. "What did he say?"

"Nothing."

"Get out your note-book, and put down, under the heading 'Trent': 'Suspicious silence.' A very bad lot, Trent. Keep him under constant espionage. It's a clue. Work on it."

Pillingshot made a note of the silence, but later on, when he and the prefect met in the dormitory, felt inclined to erase it. For silence was the last epithet one would have applied to Trent on that occasion. As he crawled painfully into bed Pillingshot became more than ever convinced that the path of the amateur detective was a thorny one.

This conviction deepened next day.

Scott's help was possibly well meant, but it was certainly inconvenient. His theories were of the brilliant, dashing order, and Pillingshot could never be certain who and in what rank of life the next suspect would be. He spent that afternoon shadowing the Greaser (the combination of boot-boy and butler who did the odd jobs about the school house), and in the evening seemed likely to be about to move in the very highest circles. This was when Scott remarked in a dreamy voice, "You know, I'm told the old man has been spending a good lot of money lately...."

To which the burden of Pillingshot's reply was that he would do anything in reason, but he was blowed if he was going to cross-examine the head-master.

"It seems to me," said Scott sadly, "that you don't *want* to find that sovereign. Don't you like Evans, or what is it?"

It was on the following morning, after breakfast, that the close observer might have noticed a change in the detective's demeanour. He no longer looked as if he were weighed down by a secret sorrow. His manner was even jaunty.

Scott noticed it.

"What's up?" he inquired. "Got a clue?"

Pillingshot nodded.

"What is it? Let's have a look."

"Sh—h—h!" said Pillingshot mysteriously.

Scott's interest was aroused. When his fag was making tea in the afternoon, he questioned him again.

"Out with it," he said. "What's the point of all this silent mystery business?"

"Sherlock Holmes never gave anything away."

"Out with it."

"Walls have ears," said Pillingshot.

"So have you," replied Scott crisply, "and I'll smite them in half a second."

Pillingshot sighed resignedly, and produced an envelope. From this he poured some dried mud.

"Here, steady on with my table-cloth," said Scott. "What's this?"

"Mud."

"What about it?"

"Where do you think it came from?"

"How should I know? Road, I suppose."

Pillingshot smiled faintly.

"Eighteen different kinds of mud about here," he said patronisingly. "This is flower-bed mud from the house front-garden."

"Well? What about it?"

"Sh—h—h!" said Pillingshot, and glided out of the room.

"Well?" asked Scott next day. "Clues pouring in all right?"

"Rather."

"What? Got another?"

Pillingshot walked silently to the door and flung it open. He looked up and down the passage. Then he closed the door and returned to the table, where he took from his waistcoat-pocket a used match.

Scott turned it over inquiringly.

"What's the idea of this?"

"A clue," said Pillingshot. "See anything queer about it? See that rummy brown stain on it?"

"Yes."

"Blood!" snorted Pillingshot.

"What's the good of blood? There's been no murder."

Pillingshot looked serious.

"I never thought of that."

"You must think of everything. The worst mistake a detective can make is to get switched off on to another track while he's working on a case. This match is a clue to something else. You can't work on it."

"I suppose not," said Pillingshot.

"Don't be discouraged. You're doing fine."

"I know," said Pillingshot. "I shall find that quid all right."

"Nothing like sticking to it."

Pillingshot shuffled, then rose to a point of order.

"I've been reading those Sherlock Holmes stories," he said, "and Sherlock Holmes always got a fee if he brought a thing off. I think I ought to, too."

"Mercenary young brute."

"It has been a beastly sweat."

"Done you good. Supplied you with a serious interest in life. Well, I expect Evans will give you something—a jewelled snuff-box or something—if you pull the thing off."

"*I* don't."

"Well, he'll buy you a tea or something."

"He won't. He's not going to break the quid. He's saving up for a camera."

"Well, what are you going to do about it?"

Pillingshot kicked the leg of the table.

"*You* put me on to the case," he said casually.

"What! If you think I'm going to squander——"

"I think you ought to let me off fagging for the rest of the term."

Scott reflected.

"There's something in that. All right."

"Thanks."

"Don't mention it. You haven't found the quid yet."

"I know where it is."

"Where?"

"Ah!"

"Fool," said Scott.

After breakfast next day Scott was seated in his study when Pillingshot entered.

"Here you are," said Pillingshot.

He unclasped his right hand and exhibited a sovereign. Scott inspected it.

"Is this the one?" he said.

"Yes," said Pillingshot.

"How do you know?"

"It *is*. I've sifted all the evidence."

"Who had bagged it?"

"I don't want to mention names."

"Oh, all right. As he didn't spend any of it, it doesn't much matter. Not that it's much catch having a thief roaming at large about the house. Anyhow, what put you on to him? How did you get on the track? You're a jolly smart kid, young Pillingshot. How did you work it?"

"I have my methods," said Pillingshot with dignity.

"Buck up. I shall have to be going over to school in a second."

"I hardly like to tell you."

"Tell me! Dash it all, I put you on to the case. I'm your employer."

"You won't touch me up if I tell you?"

"I will if you don't."

"But not if I do?"

"No."

"And how about the fee?"

"That's all right. Go on."

"All right then. Well, I thought the whole thing over, and I couldn't make anything out of it at first, because it didn't seem likely that Trent or any of the other fellows in the dormitory had taken it; and then suddenly something Evans told me the day before yesterday made it all clear."

"What was that?"

"He said that the matron had just given him back his quid, which one of the housemaids had found on the floor by his bed. It had dropped out of his pocket that first night."

Scott eyed him fixedly. Pillingshot coyly evaded his gaze.

"That was it, was it?" said Scott.

Pillingshot nodded.

"It was a clue," he said. "I worked on it."